Tracy L. Carbone

The Man of Mystery Hill

An Abby McNabb Mystery

Shakin' up
Young Readers

QUAKE

quakeme.com

THE MAN OF MYSTERY HILL
A Quake Book
Shakin' Up Young Readers!

First Quake paperback printing / August 2010

All rights Reserved.
Copyright © 2010 by Tracy L. Carbone

Cover © Nathalie Moore
Artwork © Scott Frisco

QUAKE
is a division of
Echelon Press, LLC
9055 G Thamesmeade Road
Laurel, MD 20723
www.quakeme.com

All rights reserved. No part of this book may be used or reproduced in any manner whatsoever without written permission, except in the case of brief quotations embodied in critical articles and reviews. For information address Echelon Press, LLC.

13-Digit ISBN: 978-1-59080-670-8
10-Digit ISBN: 1-59080-670-0
eBook: 1-59080-671-9

PRINTED IN THE UNITED STATES OF AMERICA
10 9 8 7 6 5 4 3 2 1

To my daughter, Abigail,
who will always be
the brightest star in my sky.

In Memory of Robert E. Stone
1929-2009
President, founder, owner of
America's Stonehenge

Chapter One

Abby McNabb fidgeted on her front steps, waiting for Dad to show up. Her best friend, Claudia Candle, a giddy nine-year-old blonde girl, sat beside her, glancing down the street in anticipation of their ride. Abby frowned with jealousy at her friend who lived two streets away with her parents, the boring and predictable Lily and George Candle.

What Abby wouldn't give to have a mom and dad a fraction as unnoticeable. Her mom, Saffron McNabb: utterly gorgeous with lush black hair and green eyes. Mom wanted to blend in, made every effort to hide her beauty behind baggy clothes and a dowdy look. She held a job as a librarian to keep a low profile.

No use. She was a knockout and couldn't even go to the grocery store without guys falling all over her. In her defense, not Mom's fault—born pretty—but it still embarrassed Abby when guys whistled at her.

Abby's father, Andy McNabb, well...too interesting. Downright weird. Obsessed with aliens, other worlds, and everything others considered fake. Except, he believed it all. Mom said it caused their divorce. Because he couldn't tell the difference between real and pretend anymore.

Lucky for Dad, tons of people believed in pretend so when he wrote a book about aliens, then another one about ghosts, he made a lot of money. Lots of people admired Andy McNabb. Not Abby though. She loved him, but wrote him off as crazy. Mom did too. Mom said the only people who didn't think he was nuts must be a little imbalanced.

Abby looked over enviously at Claudia, with her thin straight shining blonde hair, always positioned right in place. By contrast, Abby's hair was brown, thick and too curly to control. Claudia's ears: double pierced. Abby’s: not one lousy piercing. Claudia's parents: still married, and Abby's: long divorced. Abby’s jealousy bubbled up in her so strong she could taste it. Mom encouraged her to focus on good things in her life. Not an easy task when her best friend's life seemed so perfect.

Just then, Dad's car pulled into the driveway. He lived on Acorn Hill, in a brick cottage, three houses from Lily, George, and Claudia, right by the 16th hole on a golf course. Two years ago when he returned from a mysterious trip to Peru, he lucked out and found that place for sale on Lily’s street and snatched it right up. Paid cash on the spot. Some people thought it funny Dad and Mom lived just a couple of streets apart, but Abby liked it this way. Sometimes she pretended they had never split up at all.

Abby rolled her eyes as Dad's black car came into view. A giant green painted alien decorated his hood, and a bumper sticker read, "I brake for Martians." As Claudia and she started for the car, her mother called through the window, "Girls, remember, everything he says is pretend. None of it's real."

"Okay, Mom," Abby said.

"Okay, Saffron," Claudia called out.

Dad, who had the same curly brown hair as Abby, stepped out of his car. He opened the backdoor and ushered the girls into the backseat. They buckled up and he said, "Remember girls, people don't have to believe in things to make them real. Do you have to see something to believe it?" He always contradicted whatever Mom said.

They smiled. "No way, we believe everything!"

"There's my girls. Ready for an adventure today?" He spun the bright crystal that hung from his rearview mirror. *Weird, but maybe a little cool. Just a little.* "Is Chase coming? Will he be joining us on our journey today?"

"Yes, he's coming too," Abby said. "He's always wanted to see America's Stonehenge; plus he's just sitting home alone again."

Chase's parents were both lawyers who worked constantly. They left the raising and nurturing of their son to Nanny, an old thin woman with the personality of a mannequin. Since Chase was related to Abby on Mom's side, a second cousin or something, Mom and Dad included him as often as they could.

"Is it far? He's supposed to be home for supper," Abby asked.

"No, it's in Salem, New Hampshire, only about fifteen minutes from here. He's having dinner with Nanny no doubt?"

"Yup."

Dad shook his head. "All right then. Off to Chase's house we go!" Dad turned on his *Pink Floyd: Dark Side of the Moon* CD and told the girls to listen carefully to the words. "Secret messages," he said.

"Your dad is awesome," Claudia said. Abby groaned.

They drove the short route to Chase's house. He was nine like Abby and in her class at school, with the same birthday as Dad. Supposedly "a sign." Chase jumped up from his outside steps when they arrived in the alien car.

"Hi, Mr. McNabb," he said as he scooted Abby over in the backseat.

"Hi, Chase," Dad said. "You know, you can just call me Andy like everyone else. You don't have to be so formal."

"It's okay, Mr. McNabb. My mom said I have to call people Mr. or Mrs. or Ms."

"All right then. But if she changes her mind, it's okay with me. Hey, what do you kids know about America's Stonehenge?" Silence echoed through the backseat. He gave them a little more time and finally, Abby spoke.

"Lots of stones?" she guessed.

"Yup," he replied. "A whole village of stacked stones and lots of underground caves. They used to call it Mystery Hill and it's mysterious for a few reasons."

"What?" Claudia asked.

"One," he put his finger up, "no one knows for sure who built the village. It's very old and was built long before other people settled in America."

"Columbus discovered America," Claudia said. Claudia was sweet, but truth be told wasn't the brightest bulb. Abby loved her, but sometimes got frustrated when she tried too hard to appear smart, blurting out facts.

"Well," Dad said as he moved the mirror to see her face, "It really wasn't Columbus. That's what *they* like you to think." Abby rolled up her eyes to Chase. Good ole Dad, always talking about the mysterious *they*. He continued. "Lots of other people were here long before Columbus. Native Americans, Vikings, lots of others. That's why it's not called Columbia."

"Dad, who is America named after?"

"Amerigo Vespucci."

"So, he came here before Columbus?" Chase asked.

"Well, no. He landed later."

Chase looked to Abby who frowned. She hated it when her dad talked in circles. Sometimes he seemed brilliant, and other times...she hated to even think the word...crazy.

"But Columbus didn't get here first," he continued. Claudia slumped in her seat. "The second thing," he put two fingers up, "there are villages just like America's Stonehenge far away, in many parts of the world. And they're all about the same age. About four thousand years old."

"Four thousand? Wow," Abby said.

Dad moved the mirror to see his daughter's reflection. "Four thousand years old. We don't have records of anyone being here back then. So who could it have been?"

"Aliens?" Claudia asked nervously, hoping for the right answer.

"Just may be," he said. Claudia smiled to Abby and Chase.

"What's the third thing, Mr. McNabb? You said there were a few mysterious things. And a few is three," Chase said.

Dad tilted his mirror one more time to see Chase's face. "I don't have a third just yet, but I will." He paused and then said, "I have a surprise in the trunk."

"What is it?" asked Claudia.

"A magical device used to find treasures in the ground."

"A metal detector?" Abby asked.

"Close, my little conspiracy kid, but even better. Dowsing Rods." They all started to ask questions at the same time, but Dad put up his hand. "No more talking now, we're here. I'll explain it all as we go."

They pulled into the parking lot and exited

the car. Ahead of them a gift shop teetered on a leaf-covered hill. "America's Stonehenge," the sign above it read. Dad popped his trunk and took out a large stick forked in two, a giant wooden letter Y. He dug around and pulled out another smaller one.

"What are those?" Chase asked.

"These are the dowsing rods. People around the world have been using them for at least seven thousand years." He handed the small one to Chase. "You hold it like this, with the V part in your hands. Concentrate very hard on what you want to find. Aim the point at the ground like this, and think." Dad walked around in a circle. Abby thought he looked very foolish. He embarrassed her, but Chase and Claudia seemed thrilled so Abby remained silent.

"You'll feel a pull, like the pull of a magnet, when you find what you're looking for." He pretended to get yanked left then right, jerking all over. The kids watched in amazement. Then he started laughing. "Just kidding. I didn't find anything. Where was I? Oh, yes. Some people use them for water, or metal. There are even reports of using them to find missing people but I don't know if I believe it. Maybe though. You just never know."

Chase closed his eyes and walked around, trancelike, with his stick.

"Let me try," Claudia said. Chase gave her the stick. She aimed the point to the ground. "I don't feel anything," she said quickly.

"Patience, little blonde-haired girl, patience. Abby, don't you want to try?"

No, I don't want to, she thought. Bad enough doing silly things around her best friend, her cousin and her dad. But in public? "What are we looking for?" She folded her arms in defiance and refused to take the stick from Claudia. "And how can we find it with a plain old stick?"

Dad frowned. "That's not very open-minded thinking. This is hardly a plain old stick." He rubbed the bark on his adult-sized dowsing rod. "It's made of hazel wood. Anyway, what makes it special is how your mind works with it. We could pick up any stick here and it would work the same. But you have to believe."

Chase ran off with Claudia to the tree line. In a few minutes, they came back with sticks forked at the end, just like Dad's. "Will these work?" Chase asked.

"Let me see," Dad said. He closed his eyes and felt the wood. "Do you believe they'll work?"

"Yes," Chase and Claudia said together.

"Well then, they will. Abby, you take the hazel rod."

She picked up the stick from the ground where Claudia had left it. At least they all had dowsing rods. They could look silly together. "You didn't say what we're looking for though, Dad." Abby asked.

"We're looking for the answers, Abby." He said it with such seriousness, Abby felt guilty for condemning the rods as stupid. Mom always stressed Dad's belief in all the pretend stuff. He really and truly believed it. Provable or not, it was real to him. That's what mattered.

"If you believe it, Dad, so do I. Let's go guys," Abby said, suddenly enthusiastic about helping her dad.

His face lit up. "Great. Onward then. Let's go see what answers we can find!"

The kids ran excitedly toward the gift shop but Dad stayed back, caught up in looking at the falling orange, red, and yellow leaves. Suddenly he felt cold. Glacial, and more than a little scared. He zipped his coat all the way to his chin but it did no good. Chilled to the bone. The wind whistling through the trees sounded like a hundred voices calling out his name. He stared past the gift shop up the hill, wondering...so much written about Mystery Hill, now called America's Stonehenge, yet with all of his investigations he had never looked into the mysteries surrounding it. He wondered why. How had he missed it, when he lived just ten miles away? Only this week the idea to explore it came to him. Now it's all he thought about.

A ball of light suddenly whizzed right toward his head. He dove out of the way just in time, hitting the ground hard and banging his wrist. Then the ball disappeared. *What the heck?* Bright colored lights flashed around the edges of his vision and he grew dizzy but then it all faded just as quickly. He looked to the children but they had turned away. No one had seen. *Did I imagine it?* he wondered. He picked up his dowsing rod, took a deep breath for courage, and followed the children inside.

Chapter Two

They all watched the mini documentary about America's Stonehenge in the viewing room off the gift shop. Abby thought the movie interesting enough, but it didn't tell them who built the ruins. The narrator of the movie only offered suggestions: Native Americans, Vikings, Irish Monks (like priests with funny haircuts), and a New Hampshire family who lived on the site two hundred years ago.

Dad, the children, and the four dowsing rods passed through the back door of the gift shop to the little stone village to find a full barn of alpacas. Chase said they looked like llamas with wigs. Claudia tried to feed one of them a piece of gum from her pocket but the worker stopped her. They all petted the alpacas while Dad read the brochure and map of the village.

"Okay, here's what we do," he said. "Follow me up the hill and over—" He turned in circles then pointed. "There. The village should be up there. The stone structures are numbered. We'll tour the area and see if anything feels mysterious."

"Should it?" Abby asked.

"I don't know. I hope so. Wait until we get up there to use the rods. That's where the action will be."

Chase and Abby played swords with the rods and Claudia pointed hers toward the sky. Dad studied the map some more while he walked, and tried not to trip. In a few minutes, they reached the hill. "Huh," Dad said.

"What, Mr. McNabb?" Chase asked.

"I don't know. I guess I thought it would be bigger. You know, like the real Stonehenge," Dad said. Chase wrinkled his face. He probably didn't know what the real Stonehenge looked like. Abby did. She'd had the mysterious places of the world shoved down her throat since birth "Just bigger. It just looks like a bunch of regular New England stone walls all stuck together. Not very majestic. I'm not sure if we'll get any answers here."

"Maybe the dowsing rods will help, Andy," Claudia offered.

He smiled, "Maybe." Dad shivered and Abby hoped he wasn't coming down with something. "Okay, everyone put your rods down like this and concentrate. Please show me the answers."

Claudia and Chase copied him. Abby glanced around, relieved no one caught on to what they were doing. "Show me the answers," she whispered. Chase and Claudia spoke the words softly too. The three children chanted the request over and over, moving their sticks in all directions.

Dad walked to the other side of the small village, keeping the children in view. After only a few minutes, Claudia gave up. "This is no fun.

Nothing's happening."

"She's right, Abby," Chase said. "Maybe we're not magic like your dad."

"Yeah, maybe not," she sighed. "I'm going to try a little more though, just in case." She pointed the stick down, closed her eyes, and thought so hard she worried her brain might explode.

She felt someone yanking her arms so opened her eyes and prepared to tell the grabber to knock it off. But no one was there. The rod pulled her toward the stone marked with a "25" sign. She glanced back and saw Chase and Claudia looking at the sky. They didn't notice her rod actually *working*! Maybe Dad wasn't crazy after all, she thought. This sure felt real.

At the mouth of the structure, she set her rod down and then crouched and walked slowly through the tunnel. It seemed so much larger in there from the outside; there didn't seem to be an end. Suddenly the ground dropped out from beneath her and she fell, down, down, down ... but didn't crash to the ground ... just hovered in the darkness. Strobing colored lights pierced the blackness. Beautiful rainbow lights surrounded her, intertwined her arms and legs, burst through her skin. The rocks walls and dirt floor had vanished. The world as she knew it disappeared into thin air.

A loud hum wound its way into her head, deeper than her ears, into her brain. Not an unpleasant noise but voices, millions of them. Soft and loud, deep and high, all of them talking over each other, vying to tell her something terribly important.

A man with copper skin and black eyes floated close. He wore a velvet brown robe that rippled like water. His body was graceful and delicate, like a deer. Yes, thought Abby, just like a liquid deer. The most perfect deer she had ever seen. A deer man. He wore a glowing circular silver stone necklace around his broad chest.

As the man glided closer to her, the stone shone brighter, like a flashlight. Abby tried to put her hand up to shield the light, to see him, but couldn't move.

His copper hand cut through the light. It held the necklace out to her but she remained frozen. Abby tried to reach for the necklace but her arms wouldn't budge. "Abby. Abby, talk to me. Talk to me!" The deer man's voice got louder and louder and the background voices lessened. She tried to respond but couldn't. "Abby!"

Dad. She opened her eyes and looked at the crowd of people standing over her. She was lying on the ground in front of the Oracle Chamber, Site 25. A small, damp cold tunnel. "Thank God, you're all right," Dad said, hugging her.

"What happened? Where's the man?" she asked.

Dad led her from the chamber and sat her outside of it on the ground.

"What man?" he asked.

"The man down there in the cave. The deer man. And all these bright colors: red, purple, orange, blue, so many lights... and I floated. And the man tried to hand me a magic necklace; and then I woke up on the ground."

"No, Abby," Chase explained. "It didn't happen that way. We were all walking around with our dowsing rods, and then you vanished. Your dad found your stick outside the Oracle Chamber, so we all ran in and he woke you up. You must have fainted."

"I didn't faint," she shouted.

"Yes, you did," Claudia insisted. "You fainted or fell asleep. Maybe you're hungry."

Abby wanted to smack her.

"Dad, he was real. The deer man. A real guy. Or thing. Creature? Don't you believe me?" Asking the question, she suddenly knew how her dad must have felt all those times they asked him the same thing. Countless times Mom had rolled up her eyes, accused him of owning too vivid an imagination. "Daddy?" Her eyes filled with tears.

He touched the side of her face, gently. "Of course I believe you. We'll talk about it later, after you've rested a little."

A man Abby didn't know, who wore an America's Stonehenge uniform, spoke. "There's a drawing of a deer in the Oracle Chamber, a cave drawing, sort of. Maybe she saw it and imagined—"

"I didn't imagine anything and didn't see any stupid old drawing. Just go look. He must still be there," Abby demanded, pointing to the Chamber.

Claudia trotted off, ran inside and came right

back. "There's no one in there. I walked through the whole thing. It's dark and scary. No rainbows or magic men in there. You must have dreamed him up."

Dad got his daughter to her feet and handed her the small hazel dowsing rod. "Well, children, maybe there is something magical here after all. Let's go get some lunch at Friendly's and Abby can tell us all about her deer man. I have some crayons in my car. You think you can draw him? I know drawing animal legs can be a little tricky."

"He didn't really look like a deer, but was graceful and all brown. No antlers or anything. I can draw him."

"Good. Let's go then. I need some hot cocoa. I'm freezing. I want to walk out this way so we can quickly see the other side. I promise not to dilly dally."

Chase said to Abby, "You look like you saw a ghost. Did you?"

"I don't know, Chase. Something supernatural for sure though."

"Awesome."

Suddenly, something jerked at Abby's left arm. Chase and she looked down to see her dowsing rod pulling her again. "Dad!" He and Claudia spun around and gasped.

"Geez, Louise," Dad said. "Okay, just follow the rod. Let it guide you. Chase, stay next to Claudia. Don't be afraid, Abby." She held the forked stick with two hands. Dad walked beside her, making sure she didn't faint or fall. Chase and Claudia walked closely behind with their mouths hanging open. Abby trembled, a bit from fear, a bit from excitement. Scary, but fun!

Andy watched Abby with amazement. All the times he had ever used dowsing rods, the most action he got was a little tug, something that could have been his imagination. Abby's rod dragged her across Mystery Hill like a German Shepherd chasing a cat. She stopped suddenly.

"Here it is," she said.

"What is it?" Chase asked.

"Hold on, let me see," said Dad as he flipped through the site map, "The Sacrificial Stone."

"What's Sakakickle?" Claudia asked.

Normally, Dad would have laughed at her mispronunciation, but he had a bad feeling. His daughter had seen an apparition in a stone cave, and now a dowsing rod led her to this. Whatever this all meant, it couldn't be good. He tried to hide the fear closing in on him, went into teacher mode, his vocation before he became a writer. He had to be brave, for the children. "Sacrificial," he repeated. "S-A-C-R-I-F-I-C-I-A-L," spelling it out. "It means this stone was used for sacrifices." The three looked to him for more. They still didn't understand.

"A long time ago, people believed giving something they loved or needed to their god protected them. The god wouldn't hurt them and would give them what they wanted, like good weather or good crops."

"So their god just wanted to get stuff, he didn't care if they were good or not?" Chase asked.

"I'm not sure what the gods really wanted, or which ones were real. But people thought if you gave up something special, then the god would know you cared and give you a break."

"So people just left gifts on the stone?"

"Something like that, Chase. It's shaped like a table and is on stone legs so someone assumed it was; but who knows?"

Claudia kept busy mulling the new word over and over, trying to get it right. "Sakafickle. Sassafishel. Saffalickle."

Dad rubbed his hands together, trying to stop his shivering. "What do you think, Abby?" They all turned to her, waiting for an answer. Her eyes got cloudy and then the dowsing rod leapt from her hand, rose in mid-air, and flew onto the rock table. It spun around twice, split in two right down the middle of the Y, and then fell onto the ground.

Chase and Claudia's eyes grew wide as moons.

"I think it looks like a doorway," Abby said. When she said the words the corners of Andy's vision smudged, his real life peeling away to reveal blinding light and rainbows. Instead of his daughter's voice, millions of voices boomed around him, all different languages, groans and cries of animals shouting over each other, all beckoning to him. The bright lights and sound got louder and louder until his world fell away and Andy fainted.

Chapter Three

Holy Cannoli, thought Johnny Macaroon as he listened to the message on the answering machine. He assumed Saffron was home, which is why he let himself in. He planned to ask her and Abby if they wanted to get a pizza. After six years of being the lonely single neighbor, he'd become part of the McNabb family. Moved in when Andy and Saffron were still married, and they got used to having him around. Back then he'd stopped by at some point nearly every day to check in and say hello. After the divorce, Saffron gave him a key so he could water plants or enter the house in case of an emergency.

He lowered the volume button on the machine and then played it again.

"Mrs. McNabb this is Mark from America's Stonehenge. Everything's fine but your ex-husband fainted. We called an ambulance and he's okay now but we'd feel better if you came to get him. We don't want him to drive. Liability you know. We've got some kids here too. I'll try your cell phone."

Stonehenge! Johnny erased the message and sank into the couch. He had moved next door and had been hanging with Saffron and Abby all this time just so he could keep an eye on Andy and keep him away from there! Andy had no idea of the danger he had just put them both in.

Until now, Johnny had prevented Andy from making it to Stonehenge. But somehow he made it there anyway. Doomed. Darn it. Both of them doomed. They had really nice little lives now, but a trip to America's Stonehenge would change that. Andy might not care, but Johnny sure did. Well, Johnny would make sure Andy didn't go back again, and he'd just have to hope no damage was done today.

Abby cringed—well they all did—when Mom's car screeched into the parking lot and pulled in alongside the ambulance. Before she got there, right after Dad had fainted, he had woken within a few seconds looking really confused but otherwise fine. He then walked down to the exit of Stonehenge but the paramedics insisted on checking him over. They had just given him the all clear and packed up to leave when Mom pulled in.

Bundled in his coat and wrapped in a blanket, Dad still shivered.

"Do you think she's mad or worried?" Abby asked.

"Worried," he replied. "But she'll be angry later once she finds out I'm physically fine."

"What should I tell her? What happened to the two of us back there?"

"I don't know, Abby. I really don't know." He shuddered. "But I'll handle it with your mom,"

Dad said.

Mom stormed to the stone wall. Abby, Dad, Claudia, Chase and some Mystery Hill staff had promised to sit and wait there for her. When she saw Dad sitting up, seemingly unharmed, her look changed from one of concern to irritation.

"Are you all right?" Mom asked. Those were the words she actually spoke, but it came out kind of snarky, like "You're just fine aren't you? Perfectly physically fine? Just another one of your *crazy* stunts."

Dad shrugged and smiled, trying out the old charming smile that worked so well when Abby's parents were still married. Nope. Not effective anymore.

"Well?" Mom glared at him. "How about you, Abby?"

"I'm fine," Abby replied.

"Andy?"

"I'm fine, Saffron. I just got a little dizzy. I'm okay; the kids are okay. I'm just really cold."

"Well, let me take you home."

"I can drive."

"No." Mom gave him "the look," her left eyebrow pointed up painfully high. Abby often warned Mom her face would stay that way, which generally only got Mom to raise it even higher. "You are in no shape to drive. What if you crash your car?"

"I can take him home, Ma'am," one of the workers said. "My friend and I talked about it and he'll follow us in his car."

"Thank you," she said, without even consulting Dad.

Abby got angry when Mom treated Dad like a little kid, but Dad had learned to play along with it.

"It's just because she cares," Dad whispered to Abby.

"Thanks," Dad said to Mom. "Okay then, so let's hit the road."

"*I'll* drive the kids home," Mom said. "Andy, why don't you call me later?" She walked over to him and felt his forehead. "You're not warm so I guess you're all right." She picked up his chin and looked in his eyes as she moved her index finger back and forth across his field of vision. He followed with his eyes. "Still, make sure you call me later so I know you're all right. You shouldn't be this cold so maybe you've got a touch of something."

He smiled and she smiled back, just a little. "Come on kids."

Mom bombarded them with questions as soon as she started the car and they buckled up. "What happened to Daddy, Abby?" She spoke from the front seat and kept checking her mirror, just like Dad always did, to make eye contact with them.

"Nothing," Abby said. "He just fainted. I think you're right. He's got a touch of something."

"Was he seeing things again? What was he doing when he fainted?"

Chase spoke. "Just standing there; looking at us."

"No funny business going on? Any ghosts or goblins?"

"Nothing funny, no," Abby said.

"Well I don't get it then. He stood there looking at you and passed out? What on earth would upset him enough to faint?"

The kids all looked to each other. "Nothing, Mom. We just toured the site, walked around."

Claudia wriggled about, dying to tell Mom everything. Abby and Chase kept shooting her looks but it did no good. Claudia blurted out what Abby had planned to keep secret. "Abby fainted too."

Mom slammed on the brakes and all of their seatbelts grabbed their shoulders and held them tight. "What?"

"I didn't faint," Abby said.

"She did, Saffron. She wandered off and we lost her. No one could find her and Andy got really scared. But then he found her, passed out in the little cave."

"Abby, you fainted? Trapped in a cave? Are you okay?" Mom asked, now turned around. She had pulled to the side of the road and parked the car.

"I didn't faint. She's lying. And I wasn't trapped."

"Chase, what happened?" Mom asked, hoping to get to the bottom of this.

"We wandered around using dowsing rods

and um," he paused, looked to Abby whose eyes pleaded with him to lie. "And she walked to one of the rock structures and sat down. She didn't faint." He warned Claudia to keep quiet.

It didn't work. Claudia lacked the ability to lie. Darn her, Abby thought. Claudia yelled out, "She fainted and she saw a ghost who looked like a deer, and the dowsing rod dragged her across the village and then it flew up and spun around on the Sallanickel table. And then Andy fainted."

"I see," Mom said. "The dowsing rod pulled her and spun around huh? And she saw a ghost who looked like a deer?"

"Yup," Claudia said proudly. "Exactly."

Abby rolled up her eyes to her mother as if to say, "Oh come on, does that *sound* true?"

Mom smiled, "Children and their imaginations. Well, Daddy said he felt cold. Maybe he's catching the flu. Abby, you'd better hang around the house tomorrow, just in case you're catching it too."

"Why? I told you I didn't faint."

"But you did wander off and get lost. I believe a portion of Claudia's story. It's not safe to go off on your own."

"Fine!" Abby crossed her arms and frowned.

"Maybe Johnny Macaroon can come over tonight for dinner." Johnny, their neighbor, was a toy inventor. Pretty neat job, and a nice enough guy, but he tried too hard to make Abby like him. *Annoying.*

"He's strange," Abby said.

"Enough," Mom said sourly and gave her a

watch-the-attitude glance. Abby frowned more. Mom turned around and put the car in gear.

Chase cupped his hand and whispered to her, "Whatever happened I believe you." He smiled at her and soon she felt better.

Late in the afternoon, Andy sat on his couch, wrapped in a blanket in front of a blazing fire. He had dragged the couch right in front of the fireplace. He'd made himself a whole pitcher of hot cocoa and planted it on the table in a carafe beside him.

An infomercial for an upside-down tomato plant played on the TV. It got him thinking about gravity. He moved his hand up and down, studying the weight. "It's so heavy. My arm feels so heavy." He moved the fuzzy blanket off of him and lifted his foot with great effort.

"The gravity is so high here. What changed?"

The doorbell interrupted his thoughts. He managed to heave himself off of the couch, opened the door and faced a UPS driver.

He handed Andy a package. Most likely a book, he thought, based on the shape. Nearly every day, the driver, Stan, showed up at Andy's door with a box or certified letter. Andy's research never stopped, so others who'd had paranormal experiences often sent him "proof" of the extraordinary. Photos, tapes, or pieces of fabric with designs on them, which looked like Mother Teresa, Jesus, Elvis or Jim Morrison arrived continuously.

Andy signed for the package. "Stan, can I ask you as question?"

"Sure thing, Andy."

"Do you feel heavier today?" The chubby man's face reddened and he tugged at his shirt.

"Well, no, not really. I've been doing Weight Watchers with the wife you know, already lost 22.5 pounds. Haven't cheated at all. Honest."

Gulp. "I'm so sorry. I didn't mean it that way. You look great, really. I meant denser."

"What? You mean stupid?"

"Here, come in out of the cold for a minute. Come in."

Stan stepped into Andy's dining room.

"Would you like a cup of hot chocolate? I made it with pure chocolate, ninety percent cocoa from Brazil and organic sugar."

"On a diet, remember?"

Andy bopped his forehead. "What is my problem today?" Without waiting for an answer, Andy reached into a fridge and handed the man a cold can of diet root beer. Stan smiled and took it.

"This I can drink. Thanks."

"I can put it in a glass. I've got spray whipped cream."

"Thanks but no. Have to get back to my route."

"Right, right. Okay, well, I had an experience today—"

"Like the kind in your books?" Stan's eyes lit up. Stan was a big fan and Andy and he’d had many conversations about the supernatural over the years. Stan unfortunately had never seen anything out of the ordinary, which Andy attributed to the bowling ball shape of his head. He couldn't prove it, but Stan had such a big hard round head, Andy imagined it blocked any magic waves from penetrating. Still though, Stan listened intently and certainly believed in the possibility and/or reality of the events that filled Andy's days.

"Yes, just like in my books. I'm still not sure what happened today, as a lot of it is lost. Sucked right out of my memory. I just remember being really cold, and really scared. And Abby saw something too. And then I fainted."

Stan sipped his root beer down in one long gulp. "Mind if I sit?"

Andy guided him to the couch. "And now, I'm still really cold and just feel so heavy. Not fat, just heavy. I'm wondering if you've noticed a change in gravity today? Do you feel heavier?"

"No, I'm afraid I don't."

Andy slowly moved his hand up and down, as did Stan. "See, my hand; it's a lot more effort to move it up and down."

"You said you felt cold. Maybe you've got a fever."

"Nope." Andy retrieved a thermometer, which rested on the coffee table. "It's been consistently 96.9 all day and that's with the hot cocoa."

"Pretty low."

"No, 96.9 is my regular. 98.6 is an average.

Most of the people I know have temps in the 97s. There are bound to be some people out there in the 99s though to arrive at the average."

"Mine is normally 99.2."

"See? Anyway, I'm not sick."

"Good to know. But are you okay? You said you don't remember part of today, and you said you feel...heavy."

"Yes, well, I'll be all right. I just wondered if I had an anomaly or if a gravity switch occurred on the planet."

Stan frowned, looked apologetic. "Think it's just you, bud. I have to get back on my route now."

"Well, thanks for stopping in. You want a root beer for the road?"

"Let's save it for tomorrow."

"Good enough."

Andy led him out the door. He grabbed a notebook and started writing. "Very strange. Very strange indeed." He looked down at his foot, lifted it, set it down, lifted it, set it down. "Very strange."

Chapter Four

On Sunday, Abby tried everything she could to get out of being grounded, but Mom stood firm. Abby could *not* leave the house. Finally though, Abby got her to give in.

"Mom, Claudia's church is doing something fun today. It's bring-a-friend-to-church day."

"Is it really?"

"It is. Look it up online." Abby had researched the schedule, which is how she found out about the special service. Claudia confirmed it. Claudia had then been able to talk her family into going and bringing Abby along. The Candles didn't go every week, but once in a while managed to get it together on Sunday morning, if it poured rain and George couldn't play golf.

"I will," Mom said. "And I'm calling Lily."

"Go ahead. Lily and George will pick me up and drop me right off after the service."

"Right after?"

"We might go to lunch. But I promise not to enjoy it. I'll get all green vegetables or fish or something."

Mom laughed. "I suppose it's all right. You don't have to get fish. I'm not angry, but I have to set boundaries. You need to stay with adults when you're outside. And I don't believe you told me everything about yesterday. You understand?"

"Of course. I just feel really spiritual today and want to go to church."

Mom gave her "the look." Abby hadn't admitted one way or the other to fully disclosing yesterday's events. "Feeling spiritual? What exactly did happen at Mystery Hill?"

"Spirituality is a private thing," Abby replied. She had read that in an article somewhere so figured Mom would buy it. Being a voracious reader since the age of five really supplied her with some great lines.

"Okay, okay but right after lunch you come home. Then no more socializing."

"Thanks, Mom."

When Andy awoke, he felt a cool breeze under him. He rolled over and attempted to hug his pillow but—*where is it?* He opened his eyes. *My bed's gone!* He found himself hovering over the mattress, lacking proper gravity. He flipped around to stand and banged his head on the ceiling. "What the heck is going on? Another gravity shift?" he murmured.

Then—wham! —Gravity returned and just as quick and he dropped, like a load of bricks, onto his bed.

He got up, carefully. "Okay, I'm normal now. As heavy as I should be." He took a few steps, walked into his kitchen, and turned on his coffee machine. "Either I'm really losing my mind this time, or something very peculiar is happening."

He grabbed his notebook and pen and perched himself on his couch while he waited for the coffee to brew.

"Saturday, experienced too much gravity. Sunday, not nearly enough. I need to get some blood work done, see if anything inside me has changed." He scratched his head. "Though that wouldn't explain the gravity." He jumped up and ran to his scale. Stood on it and frowned. "Same as always. I'll try again later if I feel heavy or light again." The coffee maker beeped and he dashed to the kitchen.

Johnny Macaroon awoke in a bright yellow room. He loved colors. Visual stimulation was part of the fun of being human, being able to see with eyes, and not just sense colors like before. Johnny had painted each room a screaming shade of delight. The kitchen bellowed, "Praying Mantis Green," the living room, "Easter Egg Pink," and the spare bedroom, "Caribbean Blue."

He painted glow-in-the-dark stars on the ceilings and the walls, in different sizes to give the appearance of depth. He even painted them on the shades. The mostly invisible dots hid during the day, but at night Johnny switched on wall-mounted black lights to charge up the paint. When he shut the ultra violet lights off, and plunged himself into utter darkness except for a thousand points of light... *Amazing.*

Like walking through a star tunnel. He looked forward to nighttime, when he'd sit on his swivel recliner in the middle of the otherwise empty living room and spin around, stars and meteors in all directions. Except for the black spot where the wall-mounted TV rested, he drowned in endless stars and memories. He pretended the TV spot was a doorway to new realms, or old realms. He'd smile and think about other lives he had experienced before coming here, and other lives he'd have again someday when he'd be forced to leave.

No matter how appealing his bright and sunny "Burst of Sunshine Yellow" bedroom looked, in his mind, he forever drifted through the stars of eternity and memory. He needed to find out what happened at Mystery Hill yesterday, needed to talk to those kids. He couldn't go back to the stars yet, not the real ones. He preferred his glow-in-the-dark paint and vibrant walls in a sturdy little house. "Andy, please don't mess this up for me."

Abby walked into the church, and as always experienced a sense of awe. Mom told her she felt the same way, but for some reason they rarely attended. Always too busy or they slept late. A lot of times too, Abby stayed at Dad's overnight on Saturdays so Sunday mornings they did learning activities, like checking out supposed haunted restaurants or visiting museums. They made frequent trips to Salem, Massachusetts and other little and well-known mysterious New England locations.

Even when Abby and her Mom did manage to make it, this wasn't their church anyway, not their religion. The McNabbs, on the rare occasion when they entered a house of worship, or a house of understanding, which is what Mom and Dad preferred to call it, really enjoyed themselves. The McNabb's belonged to the Unitarian Universalists technically. They "believed in lots of different things and took the best from all the world religions and didn't have to explain themselves to anyone." Mom's words. Not the church's official stance.

Abby liked the encouragement of freedom of thought and being exposed to all the different belief systems and varied cultures, but there was something to be said for the Catholic Church the Candles belonged to. Everyone there believed the same basic religious things, had learned all the stories at the same ages in their religious classes. They had rituals they rigorously followed. The repetition and the collective belief of all the congregants added to this "force" in their church, which Abby didn't always get at her UU place. Abby liked her own "religion" but certainly for an occasional intense dose of unwavering belief and unquestionable structure, the Catholics nailed it.

Abby followed the Candles into the cathedral and underwent the familiar take-your-breath-away moment when she saw the enormity of the inside of the chapel. Stained glass windows, some of them uplifting and some a little too violent for her tastes, lined both sides of the church.

Everyone sat down, sliding into the cool wooden seats. *This sure beats staying home bored with Mom,* she thought.

The priest entered wearing a long black robe. He spoke in a deep voice and sang something in Latin. Of course Abby didn't know Latin, but Mom had taken a bunch of years of it back in high school and said all the time, "this word comes from the Latin word for this word," so Abby had gotten pretty used to hearing the language in snippets.

Father Morrissey didn't have a melodious voice but it still soothed Abby to hear him singing praises in a long-dead language. She'd never understand why anyone stopped speaking Latin.

When the choir got up and started singing a song whose only words were alleluia, but to a different melody than the Alleluia song in her UU church, Abby started to fade out. One minute she sat crowded on the pew with everyone, enjoying the music, in awe of the colors on the walls from the sun shining through the stained glass.

And the next, she'd traveled into her mind, the rainbow walls transformed to the rainbow world she'd been immersed in at Mystery Hill. Her heart fluttered as she recalled the way she'd felt. Yesterday's journey in the cave made her wonder if Heaven was the same. A whole existence of pure joy, color and light, and feeling.

Was there music in the special place where she had gone? Voices, hundreds or thousands or millions of voices boomed loudly. But no music.

Just chatter. What did they say? She wondered. *What did you say?* She strained to remember any glimpses of the speech, even a single word, but the memory had drifted too far away. She closed her eyes to bring back the rainbow world, feel again the way she had. Her skin prickled with excitement. The voices came back, soft at first, then louder. More of them joined and she felt herself floating on air, the ground around and under her endless waves of pastel.

"Hey, Abby, come on, it's time to go," Claudia said. "Abby, wake up."

"What?" Abby popped her eyes open. "I just dozed off for a second."

"More than a second," Claudia argued.

"But we just got here." Abby didn't recall kneeling and standing, kneeling and standing, kneeling and standing, or having to face the embarrassing part of the service when everyone but she walked up front to get Communion.

"Yeah. It's all over."

"But—"

"You fell asleep almost right away. My mom said you looked really tired and I should let you rest."

"Asleep? So I dreamt it?"

"Dreamt what, Honey?" Lily asked.

"Nothing. I just, I thought I was back at, I mean—sorry I fell asleep."

"It's okay, Claudia falls asleep here sometimes too."

"Do you think I could just go home? Skip

going out to lunch and just eat at my house? Maybe my mom is right and I'm coming down with something."

Mrs. Candle agreed to bring her home, and within minutes, Abby walked in her front door, still trying to figure out what the heck had just happened, worried her mind was slipping away.

The rest of the day went smoothly with Abby doing everything she could to get her mind off of her little trip into the unknown yesterday, and then this morning's repeat performance. Abby felt frightened about what was going on in her head and wanted her mother close.

To Mom's delight, Abby helped her to clean the house, accompanied her to The Christmas Tree Shop (which Mom said served as an exception to the grounded rule because she knew Abby hated the store as much as Mom loved it) and even helped her make lasagna for dinner. After dinner, through which Abby could not stop thinking about her visions, she politely excused herself to do some research on her computer. Maybe if she looked up Mystery Hill, she'd find other people who saw weird things there too, and she'd feel better. Up in her room, behind a partially closed door, she looked up America's Stonehenge and Mystery Hill, its two names. Just when it looked like she had finally found something helpful, Mom called her downstairs.

"What," she yelled.

"Come on down. Johnny's here and wants to

test out a new game."

Abby frowned. She was on a roll but couldn't pass up a game testing night. "Be right down." She printed a bunch of pages and set them aside to read later.

A couple of minutes later, Abby sat at the dining room table with Johnny and Mom and looked over the prototype for one of the games he had designed. He would be presenting this game and others to a toy company on Friday. Though just a rough model of the game, it was all the company would need to grasp how to play it. If they liked it, the company would build a real model later. Abby liked being what he called his focus group. Claudia, Chase and she usually got to test all of his games and toys before he showed them to anyone else.

"So you pick up a card and move your guy three spaces and AARGH – the monster grabs you from under the bed. What do you think?"

Abby looked at the yellow fuzzy arm with orange spots shoved onto a Popsicle stick, the "monster arm" which would leap out at players if they tripped the mechanism on the board. "Where did you get that arm? Is it Muffy's arm?" Muffy, a stuffed kitty Abby got when she was two years old but hadn't seen in over a year seemed to have unwittingly given up a limb. Many of Abby's old toys donated parts for Johnny's games and puzzles. She usually didn't mind because she liked to be a part of the inventing process—but Muffy?

Johnny looked to Mom then to Abby. "I don't know. It was in a box your mom gave me. I needed the arm. I can sew it right back on after Humbro sees the game. It's just a model. I'll give it back Friday, okay? Here let's play the game." He handed her a card and smiled at her apologetically. "Sorry, okay?"

She wanted to be angry with him, but his big goofiness made it tough. Plus, she had to admit his toy inventing impressed her. Last year he managed to get her and Claudia's picture on the back of a box for a game he invented. Mom gave her teacher one and now it sat proudly on the shelf of her classroom.

"As long as you put it back," she said.

"Friday, I promise." Then he smiled from way up high—he was wicked tall even when sitting down.

They played the game for a while. Abby enjoyed it and told him other kids would too. Johnny wanted to play a video game but Abby said she needed to go upstairs to read.

"Don't forget to call your father," Mom reminded.

"I won't."

Andy stepped on the scale and then ran into his office and typed the result onto a spreadsheet. He clicked some keys and a graph appeared with a flat line.

"Nothing. All day, nothing. I don't get it."

The sound of his phone ringing made him

jump. Generally, this happened because he lingered pretty deep in thought and normal sounds like doorbells or ringing phones acted as abrupt jolts back into reality.

"Hello?" he said.

"Hi Daddy."

"Abby, hi. How was your day?"

"Good. How was yours?"

Ooh, how to answer, he wondered. Did he tell her about his strange dreams—if they could be blamed on dreams and not mental lapses or steps into a very strange place—or just wait until he knew more. "Pretty quiet. How about your day?"

Ooh, how to answer, she wondered. Did she tell him about her strange dreams—if they could be blamed on dreams and not mental lapses or steps into a very strange place—or just wait until she knew more. "Pretty quiet here too. I'm going to just relax and read a little."

"Yeah, me too. Call me tomorrow okay?"

"Sure will. I love you, Daddy."

"Love you too, Ab."

She hung up and turned to her printed pages. She was eager to find out more about America's Stonehenge and the doorway they called The Sacrificial Stone. See if they could explain her weird experiences.

When she sat on her bed and began reading, she realized they had missed a lot of stuff at the site. Large stones surrounded the site but Dad hadn't even noticed. The stones made a huge calendar. Information about stars and their alignment filled pages, but some of the words appeared large and in bold. **ARCTURUS** and **IZAR** and **BOÖTES**. She wondered why those words stood out. Sirius and Ursa Major were listed too but only **ARCTURUS, IZAR** and **BOÖTES** showed large each time. She sneezed and when she opened her eyes back up, all the names reverted to unbolded, uncapitalized and in similar font. "Weird," she said. She closed and opened her eyes again. The words remained the same size. *Show me the answers*, she thought. **ARCTURUS, BOÖTES** and **IZAR.** All capitals and very dark. She wrote down the three names to look up later.

She felt a little frightened so decided to flip to the next page. What she saw made her gasp: a photo of a stone much like the Sacrificial Stone, but standing up with a man carved into it. To Abby, it was obvious the man walked through a doorway. "I knew it," she said to herself.

The caption under the picture said, "Shutesbury, Massachusetts." It went on to explain why archeologists believed this Massachusetts stone to be another sacrificial table. Clearly, it stated, a man carved into the stone indicated that at some point in history, humans placed other humans on stones and sacrificed them to their gods.

"It's not a table. It's a gateway. Duh."

"What did you say, Abby?" Mom asked. She

walked into her room with an armful of laundry.

"Oh, nothing, I'm just researching some stuff on America's Stonehenge; you know, since we didn't get to see it all yesterday."

Mom set the clothes on her bed. "Well, that's good. Always nice to hear you're learning. I found this in the pocket of the jeans you wore yesterday. It's pretty. Did Daddy give it to you?"

Abby stared at the silver stone on the chain, dangling from her mother's index finger. Not glowing, but otherwise the stone of the deer man. No doubt. "Um, yeah, Daddy gave it to me."

Mom looked at it up close. "Is it some kind of crystal? I see little triangles in it, but it looks like metal. Huh, and it's warm. That's strange."

"I'm not sure what it's made of," Abby said as she reached for the necklace. "He didn't get a chance to say before he fainted."

"You'll have to ask him and let me know what it is. I've never seen anything like it before." Mom handed her the necklace and then put her daughter's clothes away. "I'll call you down at seven-thirty. Johnny rented another *Star Wars* movie."

"Okay, Mom." As soon as she left, Abby clutched the warm stone in her hands. She closed her eyes. "Show me the answers," she whispered. The stone grew warmer and in her mind she saw and heard the deer man again.

"Abby, I am Raphael, from the land of Gibeon. You must help your father to remember where he came from." Abby popped open her eyes, relieved to be in her room. Her heart raced *boomboomboom*. She threw the stone onto the bed, covered it with her pillow, and ran downstairs.

"What is it, Abby," Mom asked. "What's the matter? Johnny!" He came running and they both looked at the little girl, red and shaking. Johnny held the rest of Muffy, who now had a band-aid covering the hole where an arm used to be.

"Abby, you look like you saw a ghost," he said, clutching the one-armed stuffed cat close.

"I'm okay," she said. But her voice quivered and her heart beat so loudly, she couldn't hear. *Boomboomboom*. "Is Daddy really crazy?" she asked her mother.

"Well, he sees things differently than most other people," Mom explained carefully.

"If I see things, will I have to move out too? Will you think I'm crazy?" Her eyes filled with tears. Mom hugged her.

"Are you seeing things?" Johnny asked.

"Maybe I should take her to a therapist," Mom said to Johnny.

"Abby, what did you see?" Johnny asked.

"When I closed my eyes, I saw the ghost guy from yesterday. He said I need to help Dad remember where he came from."

"Abby," Johnny said calmly, "yesterday when you saw him, were your eyes closed then too?"

"I think so. Maybe."

"Do you think maybe you got carried away with your imagination because your dad wanted you to see a ghost or something magic?"

"Maybe." Abby felt hopeful. Maybe just her imagination.

Abby knew Mom prayed she wouldn't choose the same route as Dad and suddenly become obsessed with the world of make believe.

"See, nothing to worry about," Johnny concluded. "No ghost and no one talked to you. You dreamt it."

"Yeah, probably." She turned to Mom. "Where is Daddy from?"

"Bradfield, born and raised. See, your ghost doesn't know what he's talking about. You can ask Mimi and Grampy about it if you want. They'll confirm it." Mom was talking very fast, which happened whenever she got nervous.

"Okay. I'm just gonna skip the movie though and go to bed early. I'm kind of tired." Abby kissed them goodnight and walked up the stairs to her room. She didn't feel relieved like they did. Johnny explained away the ghost but he didn't know about the necklace.

She brushed her teeth, put on her pajamas, and then walked into her room to sleep. The stone peered from underneath the pillow, calling to her. *I can't sleep. Scared or not, I have a mission.*

Andy paced back and forth in his office, chewing his lip and muttering to himself. "Ah, yes," he said, and scribbled notes in a pad. Then he paced some more, scribbled some more. He sat down in his leather swivel chair in front of his laptop.

"But why—" He shook his head. "No, no, no. Abby did see something, I'm sure of it. I should call Saffron, let her know. No, that's the worst thing I could do." He chewed his lip some more. "She won't believe Abby has special abilities any more than she ever believed I did. Poor kid though, she must be terrified." He put his fingers on his temples and closed his eyes. "It's okay Abby, there's nothing to be afraid of."

Abby thought of her dad, imagined him sending her a big hug from his house. It gave her the strength she needed to pick up the phone and dial Chase's number. His Nanny answered and called him to pick up.

"Chase, can I come over tomorrow after school? Oh, and can I bring Claudia too? We can all walk home together."

"Let me ask my mom. She's in her office so I'll call her cell from my cell. Hold on," he said.

Abby hummed a song while she waited.

Chase returned, said yes, then goodbye and hung up.

Next Abby called Claudia. Lily said okay so Abby shouted down the stairs. "Mom, Claudia and I are going to Chase's tomorrow after school, okay? Lily and Amanda said okay!"

"That's fine, Abby," Saffron called out.

Satisfied she wouldn't have to be on this mission alone, Abby crawled under her covers.

Her hand retrieved the warm stone from under the pillow and held it tight. She closed her eyes and saw Raphael again, surrounded by brilliant colors, wearing his flowing brown robe. "Don't be afraid, Abby. I'm here to help. Let me tell you about your father's world."

Behind her eyelids, a movie played in 3-D. Sites and sounds and smells and feelings like nothing Abby had ever experienced before, coursed through and around her. Without words, she saw and identified stars and planets as she raced at impossible speeds through constellations that sparkled like rainbows. Without words, Raphael made her understand the evolution of the Gibeon existence, so immensely different from the humans. Without words, and in the safety of the dream realm, he showed the land of Gibeon, a wondrous world of magic that carried her off to sleep long before the clock stuck eight.

Chapter Five

The unnaturally tall, burly man with curly hair and glasses sat on Lily Candle's couch and feigned reading the newspaper while he waited for her to get the hanging wire.

"I really appreciate you hanging this painting for me, Johnny," Lily said. "I've been waiting for George to hang it for weeks and nearly hired a handyman."

"No problem. Always happy to help."

Lily grinned as she dug through what she called her junk box. "George isn't very handy, you know, bless his heart."

What an understatement, thought Johnny. George Candle liked to dress up in a suit and tie and sell copy machines but he couldn't use a tool set to save his life.

"I'm only a few streets away and it's nice to get out of my living room sometimes." Honestly, Johnny had been trying to find an excuse to come over and pump Claudia for information about what had happened at Stonehenge. He'd practically driven here shoeless when Lily had called, especially after Abby's meltdown at her house. Suddenly watching a movie over there when Abby had obviously started finding things out made him itchy to talk to Claudia. Just dumb luck that Lily called his cell and he had a reason to bolt from the McNabb's over here.

"You know what, I think the wire is in a box in the basement. Be right back," Lily said.

From the couch, Johnny could hear Claudia walking around upstairs. He knew she'd be down eventually. Per his weekly custom, George visited his elderly mother in a nursing home. Johnny had a couple of hours to get Claudia to talk before he returned, but wished she'd hurry up and come down.

In the meantime, he continued to look at the newspaper. He had no idea what he read but let his eyes dance over the black and white words printed across the page. Johnny excelled at faking being human, but never could grasp how to read like they could. The pictures and headlines made a story but guessing the content was tough.

Claudia finally skipped down the stairs and into the room, wearing flannel pajamas in a pink leopard print. She smiled then plopped herself on the opposite couch. She picked up the clicker but Johnny stopped her before she could turn on the TV and get lost in a program.

"Claudia, can you read this? My glasses aren't working tonight," Johnny asked.

She walked over and scanned the paper. "It's a lot of words. I don't know, something about a war. Looks depressing."

"Yeah, that's what I thought too." Johnny Macaroon liked Claudia. Cute and friendly and always told the truth. A great source of information.

"What have you been up to lately?" *Come on, tell me all about Stonehenge.*

She froze, "Nothing." Her fingers pulled on her hair.

Aha! Hiding something. "Nothing huh?"

"No. I have to go to bed now." She started to scurry away on her scrawny little legs.

"Claudia?" The girl stopped in her tracks. *What an obedient child*.

"What?"

"It's still early. Not bedtime yet. Come sit over here on the couch and tell me what's new." Johnny saw her glancing around for her mother, but Lily continued to rifle through the toolbox in the basement.

"Well, me, Chase, and Abby and her Dad went to Mystery Hill." Her voice lifted. *Yes, there was something here. Something helpful.*

"And?"

"And Abby fell in a cave and fainted and she said she saw a deer man. Then her dowsing rod went flying up in the air and guess where it landed?"

"Where?" Johnny Macaroon's fingers clenched and crumpled the *Bradfield Eagle.*

"The Sacalittle Stone. Only Abby said it was a doorway and not a table at all."

Johnny started to sweat. "Do you mean the Sacrificial Stone?"

"That's what I said."

His darn human body wouldn't stop sweating.

His hands shook. "Abby's dowsing rod landed on the stone huh?"

"Yup."

"What did Andy say when he woke up?"

"Nothing."

"What did he think about it being a doorway?"

"Nothing. I told you he fainted and when he woke up he didn't remember a thing."

"Oh, good. So I guess you won't go there again huh?"

"No way. Not a very fun day at all."

Did Andy remember? Johnny hoped not. Once he remembered, Johnny could kiss this human life goodbye.

"Can I go upstairs now?"

"Sure."

He'd have to keep a close eye on Andy. If he went back to Mystery Hill there could be a serious problem. It couldn't happen. He had to stop him. Now. He leapt from the couch just as Lily walked up with a handful of wire.

"Got it. I think I'd like to hang the painting over there. I'll get you a ladder."

"Don't need one," Johnny said impatiently. "Quickly, just hand me that wire and a hammer."

Andy sat at his desk staring at a glass of ice water. It had been sitting awhile and now had gray condensation on the outside and droplets racing down the sides. He leaned in close and tapped one of the ice cubes, enjoying the faint "clink" sound it made against the glass.

He picked up the drink and guzzled it. "Nope, didn't help. Still feel off."

He squinted at the walls, got up and traced his fingers against the textured fabric wallpaper. Caressing surfaces made Andy smile. Always did. Saffron used to tease him because when he tensed up, he'd touch things, anything within reach, but preferably items with a lot of texture, and he'd calm right down.

As always, it worked. As his fingers traced the grooves, his heart slowed, his breathing became even. For now, he relaxed. But he needed to get to the bottom of this anxiety. Andy knew his tension meant he was closing in on some big discovery, a breakthrough. He could feel it in every cell of his body. Normally he'd be giddy with anticipation of what the next day would bring, but Abby's involvement skewed this situation. He only hoped and prayed whatever force he neared zoning in on proved friendly. He chewed his lip and sat down to type some notes into his computer to research Mystery Hill from a different angle.

After Johnny quickly hung the painting on Lily's wall he said goodbye and headed to his car. Once he saw Lily's figure move from the window though, he ducked away from his vehicle and snuck, as much as such a large man can sneak, to Andy's home down the road. He peered through his window and spied him staring at the computer monitor. Johnny squinted and could see the words, but of course couldn't read any of them. *I can speak the language of any life form but darn it, I can't learn to read. Well, no use whining about it.*

He had to stop Andy from seeing whatever showed on his screen. For the tenth time in the last couple of years, Johnny yanked the cable wire out of the outside wall. The computer screen went funny and Andy threw his hands up. Then he shut the computer off and walked to the phone. No doubt he was calling the cable company. Johnny smirked. That would keep him from getting new information until they came in the morning to put the cord back.

But how to keep him from leaving? Hmm. Johnny looked around. Aha! He knelt down beside Andy's car and unscrewed all the valve covers then stuck a pen in the holes to release the air from all four tires.

Johnny wiped his sweaty brow and then stole in the darkness back to his car to return home to Cherokee way.

Chapter Six

Abby walked the tile floors of Bradfield Elementary trying to keep her sneakers from squeaking. SQUEAK SQUEAK. She slowed her steps. SQUEAK. Quickened her pace. SQUEAK. She bit her lip, *darn feet*. Already her second pair of new sneakers this year and Mom said she no more until her feet grew. The problem stemmed from Abby's feet though, not shoes, and they both knew it. Not a major deal as things went, because Abby knew she was cute enough, hopefully turning pretty like Mom some day. She had enough money and was healthy, so counted her blessings. Dad said she inherited his squeaky foot gene but he outgrew it. She assumed he made the story up to alleviate her concerns, and it did, but right now humiliation filled her as she walked to class. As if being worried about all this Gibeon business wasn't enough.

"Hey, Abby McSqueaky!"

Abby slammed on her brakes at the glass shattering horrible voice of Oleander Montague. She spun around and looked at the prematurely tall, red headed girl. Red freckles overran her chalky white skin, as if someone with a mouthful of strawberries sneezed on her.

"It's Abby McNabb."

"Heard you had quite the adventure Saturday. Daddy and daughter taking turns fainting at Stonehedge."

"Stonehenge. And where did you hear that?" Abby's face burned and it took all her resolve not to walk up to Oleander and pinch her. Hard.

"*The Bradfield Eagle*. Had to search for it. Didn't make the front page but I found it all right."

"Oleander, don't you have anything better to do with your time than follow me around day after day?"

With the smarmiest look Abby had ever seen, Oleander said, "Well your father is a famous author and all, big celebrity in our little nothing of a town. What other fun is there around here but to see what silly things you two get yourself into?"

"Maybe you could worry about your own father."

"Nothing remarkable about him, I'm afraid. Not like yours." She laughed and Abby thought she sounded like a hyena.

"How very boring for you."

Oleander scrunched her face and all her freckles scurried together like a bunch of red ants attacking a strawberry shortcake. "Better boring than embarrassing."

"My dad is not an embarrassment. Take it back!"

By this time a few kids had gathered round. Oleander was at her best, or her worst rather, with an audience.

"See any aliens lately? My dad said your Dad's newest book is a real hoot."

"A hoot? He said it's a hoot?" Abby clenched her fists tight, and her jaw.

Abby's pendant began to burn. She put her hand over it. Raphael's soothing voice hummed in her mind. *Ignore her, Abby. Let it go. Words can't hurt.*

"Yes, yes they do hurt," she replied. Except of course no one could hear Raphael.

"Whoever are you talking too, Abby McNabby?" Oleander giggled.

The other children laughed too. Chase walked around the corner then. "What's going on?" he asked Abby.

Oleander turned beet red. Red freckles on a red face and she looked like—

"Diaper rash face here made fun of me and my dad."

That really got the other kids laughing. Chase laughed too which made Oleander turn almost plum colored. Oleander had harbored a crush on Chase since kindergarten.

"I-I just—" she stuttered.

"What? You just what?" he asked her.

He turned to Abby, leaving crimson Oleander speechless, for once. "She's just jealous of you, Ab. Your dad is the coolest parent around and she knows it." He looked at Oleander and she stood silently waiting. Then, as if Oleander didn't exist, he glanced back to Abby. "Some people are just mean inside and out and there's nothing you can do about it. She's a bully." A few of the kids in the circle nodded agreement.

"Come on, Ab. Let's go to class."

Chapter Seven

All three children left the school and started the long walk through the woods to Chase's house. They kicked crisp leaves and Claudia lifted a few up in search of salamanders but found only black slime underneath. She wiped it on her white winter jacket and Abby giggled. Lily would be scrubbing that out later.

"So, you're telling us your dad is an alien?" Chase glared at Abby, waiting for her to respond.

Abby moved her hand to her neck and rubbed the stone. "Well, yes and no."

"I don't get it," Claudia said. "I thought aliens were green. Your dad is *not* green."

"He's not an alien! I don't even know if the green ones are real." Abby clenched her fists. "Ugh! It's complicated!" Abby stomped her feet on some broken twigs and huffed her way toward Chase's place.

"Okay, why don't you tell us again, slowly," Chase said. He had a pen ready and wrote on his hand.

Abby turned around and stopped to repeat everything Raphael had told her last night as she slept. "Well, I don't know if I remember it all, and he didn't tell me everything. He said it would take a long time to grasp. But I know my dad came from a star called Gibeon and that he showed up here on Earth, at Mystery Hill."

"No one can live on a star, Abby. They'd burn up," Chase explained.

"Just write it," she said as she commenced walking again. "You're right. Things with bodies can't live on stars, but the beings of Gibeon, the Gibeons, are..." She struggled to remember what Raphael had told her. "Energy."

"What does that mean?" Claudia asked. She held a small pile of sticks.

"Where did you get that?" Abby asked, suddenly frightened.

"I don't know. Over there. It's like a spider web. Isn't it unusual how all the sticks fell together this way? Looks like they got stuck together with grass."

"Give it to me." Abby yanked it from her friend's hand. "These didn't just get stuck together. My dad made them. They're good luck charms and have to stay right where he put them."

Chase and Claudia looked at her like she was nuts. She didn't blame them.

Claudia pointed. "I got it over there."

Abby set it down in its place. "Okay, where was I?"

"Screaming about a pile of sticks," Chase said.

"I'm sorry. My dad is very particular about those little twig shapes. He comes out to this field here for star gazing sometimes and he's always saying they have to be placed just so, or else."

"Or else what?" Claudia asked.

"Just please, don't touch them again."

"Geez, I won't." Claudia scrunched her face.

"Okay, what was I talking about?" Abby asked, eager to get back on topic.

"People with no bodies."

She smiled. Crazy but true.

"We have bodies and you can touch us right?" Abby explained, facing them. Claudia nodded. "And we have thoughts and feelings, right?" Claudia nodded again. "Okay, so these Gibeons only have thoughts and emotions, all good emotions like love and joy, but no bodies."

"How can they not have bodies?" Chase asked.

"I don't know. It's just how they are. They're balls of energy with lots of happiness."

"Weird," Chase said.

"No, Chase, just different. We can't live without oxygen, right?" Chase and Claudia agreed. "Well, the Gibeons don't need oxygen because they don't breathe, but they need the magnetic pull of their star. The metal in their star keeps them alive, keeps them all together."

Andy stirred a pot of chili, took a big whiff and smiled. "Yummy. But it still needs a little time to simmer."

He sat down at his desk and typed a few things on the computer, read the monitor, and then picked up a notebook and pen. He put on a light jacket then opened the slider to his side yard.

A weathered wooden table and chairs rested on a large brick patio. Andy sat down, clicked his pen open and began to write. After a few minutes, he looked up, smiled, nodded at the air then started writing again. "Certainly is a nice autumn night. I'd say I have about a half hour then I can eat my chili. Sure smells good."

Abby continued despite the confused looks on the faces of her two best friends. "Four billion years ago, their star exploded and pieces of it drifted through space as meteorites. Gibeons stayed with whatever piece they happened to be near when it blew up. One of those meteorites hurled toward Earth, breaking in more pieces before it landed."

"Did it land at Mystery Hill?" Claudia asked.

"No. On the other side of the world. Raphael wouldn't tell me more."

Chase scribbled something on his hand.

When Abby stopped short, he slammed into her and Claudia slammed into him. "What are you doing, Ab?" he grunted.

Her heart beat like crazy and she froze when she looked ahead. "That tree." She managed to breathe with difficulty. She pointed a shaking finger.

"The tree? You're afraid of a tree?" he asked.

Abby looked at it. Yes, as silly as it sounded, yes. Gray and gaunt and maliciously tall. Two long gnarled branches reached out, grabbing like greedy arms. Knots formed a menacing face. The roots looked like octopus legs and the lines in the bark looked like veins. Dad's good luck twig charms all around it did little to make her feel safe. The tree always spooked Abby and she usually made a point to take another route around it, by the friendly pine tree. But today she forgot.

"Hello, Abby," Claudia said, taunting her. "It's *just* a tree."

"It looks like a scarecrow someone turned to wood. I don't like it." She turned away and raced in another direction.

"You're a weird girl. You know that, Abby McNabby?" Chase called out.

"It's McNabb!"

Chase followed her. "It's just a tree, Ab. You need to relax. Let's forget about it. It's way back there now."

He smiled at her and her heartbeat slowed down a little. "Abby, what is that stone on your neck? I know it's from Raphael, but what is it?"

She rubbed her fingers over its warm surface. "It's a piece of Gibeon meteorite."

Claudia scrambled closer. "Is someone living on there, like *Horton Hears a Who?* Hello! Anybody in there?" She tapped the necklace.

"Stop it, Claudia. No one lives on it. And what's in your hand?"

Claudia shoved something behind her back. "Nothing."

"Claudia O'Hara Candle, if that's another twig spider web thing, you are in so much trouble."

She stood firm. "It's not. It's a little twig tee-pee. A little house, see?"

She held up the pile of sticks, wound together on top to make a triangle. "Maybe little Indians live in it."

"It's a different shape but it's another good luck charm. Please don't pick up any stick things you see, okay?"

"Okay!"

"Now, go put it back exactly where you found it or else," Abby snarled. Claudia walked away around the corner without asking "or else what." Good thing too because Dad never told Abby what the "or else" meant.

Flustered, Abby strained to get back to her explanation. Whose dumb idea was it to walk through these woods? Not too much longer to the back of Chase's house though. "Okay, the stones, like this one on my necklace, act like doorways for them to travel from their world to ours. The bigger the piece, the bigger the doorway. A small one like this lets me to speak to Raphael. Bigger ones let the Gibeons come right though."

"Must be a big one at Mystery Hill then, if your dad walked through," Chase said. "Because he's pretty big."

"You're right. Raphael didn't say how Dad got here, but there must be a piece of the Gibeon Meteorite at Mystery Hill." Abby's face lit up, finally understanding. "That's what the Sacrificial

Stone is! I knew it! A gateway! It must be made of Gibeon, or there must be Gibeon near it somewhere. It's why someone carved a man on the piece they found in the other town I saw online, to show us it's a doorway from there to here. Sacrificial Stone, hah! What were those archeologists thinking?"

"So if your dad came through a gateway at America's Stonehenge how did he get a human body? Was born there? Did his mother give birth to him right there, right by the alpacas?" He looked to Abby, knowing the answer. He wrote something else on his hand. "One more question. What did Raphael say about the stars whose names popped up on your paper?"

"I forgot all about those. I didn't ask."

Chase scribbled one last thing in his hand, having to use the back of it and his fingers to fit in all the notes. "Okay, this is what we have so far:

- Gibeon blew up.
- No bodies, don't die.
- Grabbed star pieces
- Chunks landed far away
- Mr. McNabb is a Gibeon
- Came through Stonehenge.
- Stars."

He looked up. "Right?"

Abby opened a small bag of M&Ms and poured them in her hand and into Chase's ink-free hand. She crunched a couple then answered.

"They didn't grab anything. They just stuck like magnets."

"Hey, where's Claudia?" Chase asked.

"She went to put the twig thing back."

"Yeah, but she's not back yet. Claudia!"

As much as she dreaded it, Abby knew she needed to run back to the creepy scarecrow tree. It only took a minute then she stood in front of it. Her mouth hung open and the crunched M&Ms fell out of her mouth.

Claudia stared glassy-eyed at the tree. Scary enough on its own, now a hologram of Raphael floated in front of the tree, had become part of it. His lips moved and he waved his hands but Abby couldn't hear anything except the wind and the rustle of branches.

She managed to look at Chase who had covered his eyes.

Then the spirit left and it reverted to being a mere tree again. Claudia looked at them. "Wow! So cool," she said.

Abby managed to close her mouth finally but most of her candies had fallen into the dirt.

Chase uncovered his eyes. "Are you okay, Claudia?"

"I'm fine. He explained everything."

"The tree?" Abby asked.

"No. Duh. Raphael. He told me so I'd understand. Come on, I'll tell you." Still in shock, Abby didn't protest when Claudia took the bag of M&Ms from her and dumped the rest into her dirty hands. She didn't even yell at her when she spit in her hands to make the colors come out on her palm.

The kids walked as quickly as they could from the tree, in no particular direction except away.

"He said Gibeons want to help people to stop fighting. Says there's a better way." She opened her hand and showed them the pretty colors from the melted candy shells. "Pretty, huh?"

"If there's a better way, then why don't the Gibeons just tell everyone what it is, show everyone how it's done?" Chase said.

"They've tried lots and lots of times. But people are scattered all over the place and most of them won't listen."

"And?" Raphael was *her* ghost and she didn't particularly like Claudia all of a sudden getting messages too.

"Gibeons couldn't travel far from their stones to talk about peace. Had to stay close to their anchors. They also couldn't just wait for people to walk by, so a long time ago Gibeons asked some humans to carry big stones all over the world and spread them out. Lots of gateways. It helped to get their peace messages out a little but it's a pretty big planet."

"I have no idea what you mean," Abby said. "If they can just ask people to move rocks, then why can't they just explain their super-special peacemaking plan?" she rolled her eyes up.

"I still don't get how Ab's dad can be a Gibeon," Chase added.

"Me either," Claudia admitted. "Just because I

talked to the tree, doesn't mean I understand it either." Her long blonde-lashed eyes filled with tears and Abby felt sorry.

"I think it's time to bring my Dad into the mystery. Agreed?" Abby put her arm out.

"Agreed," Claudia said, placing her hand down on Abby's.

"Agreed," Chase said, completing the three-way handshake. "Let's go to his house and surprise him. I'm not walking by that tree again."

"Me neither. Ever," Abby said.

Abby may have been rattled when the tree came to life, but her fear didn't come close to Johnny's. When Claudia picked up the twigs the first time, Johnny almost had a heart attack. Thank goodness Abby put it back. Then the second time, whew, Johnny really freaked out. He followed Claudia to make sure she put them back in the exact right place. She didn't of course, but before he could straighten it, Raphael appeared.

Johnny fell back against a rock and hyperventilated. Though Raphael spoke only to Claudia, and the other kids only saw him, he looked right at Johnny. Right at him!

A horrible glare of disappointment, worse than any mean look, Johnny thought. Johnny stopped being afraid and instead became sick with himself for letting Raphael down.

When the other kids came and Raphael disappeared, Johnny didn't waste any time putting the twig triangle house back where it belonged. Then he propelled those giraffe long legs as fast as they could go. Like Chase, he vowed never, ever to go in those woods again.

As the kids walked to Andy's they all caught their breath. Chase's notes had washed away with sweat and M&Ms. Abby knew they'd all memorized the notes.

Claudia didn't fear the tree, but Chase and Abby couldn't wait to get out of those woods. They both tried to act brave, but it didn't do much good. Terror ripped through them. Claudia on the other hand rattled on like seeing a ghost pop out of a scarecrow tree was nothing out of the ordinary.

"Raphael said Andy had a really important job to do and walked through a door from Gibeon to here a long time ago to do the job; but once he got here he forgot. So we need to make him remember, so he can do his new job."

"What is his job? Did Raphael say?" Abby asked as she ran alongside her.

"He's going to be soul collector."

"A what?" Chase asked.

"Specially trained Gibeons jump into human bodies to give them peace messages then jump right out and back to their stone. Problem is, sometimes when they get inside they forget who they are and think they're people. A soul collector is supposed to track them all down and send all the trapped Gibeons back because they're not allowed to stay inside."

"Wow, my dad's a soul collector. Cool."

"And an alien. Even cooler."

Abby groaned. "Thanks for the reminder."

"So why did Abby's dad get stuck?"

Claudia started playing with her hair as she looked over at the side of Dad's house. She got all glassy-eyed. Abby looked in the same direction and almost screamed when she saw Raphael's see-through body floating there. Chase covered his eyes again. Abby closed her eyes tight too and when she opened them, he'd left.

Claudia didn't seem at all rattled. The upside to being not the brightest bulb, Abby thought. Claudia finished talking. "Raphael said the human he jumped into moved away from the anchor too quick."

"Why do we see keep seeing Raphael all over the place?" Abby squeaked out. "There's no Gibeon around here except on my neck, and it's little."

"Raphael is the leader so he has more power. Anyway, I only see him when I'm near you. Bottom line, we need to help Andy remember so he can bring the other Earth Gibeons home."

"What's an Earth Gibeon?" Chase asked.

"One that gets stuck in a human. Duh," Claudia said.

"Why though? Why can't they stay?" Abby asked.

"There are humans underneath. I'm sure they'd like their lives back," Claudia explained.

"Yeah, true," Chase said.

"Not only that," Claudia said, "But if all the Gibeons return to their anchors, they'll have a lot more power and then they can help our world. When they're all spread out, like now, they're pretty weak so our world is a mess, Raphael said. Once they get all together, Earth will be a harmonica place." She beamed.

"You mean harmonious," Abby said.

"That's what I said. Peace and harmonicas all over the world."

Abby and Chase smiled at each other.

"We're here." They walked around the front of the yard.

Halfway across the lawn, a horrible realization stabbed Abby. If all the Gibeons got sent back, she would lose her father! *No, I will not let that happen!*

But when Chase knocked on the door and she saw her dad face to face, she grumbled and admitted to herself that another dad, her *very real* Earth father lived underneath, probably dying to get out and talk to her. Yup, she had to help. For the Gibeons, for the world and for the two fathers who resided in the body of Andy McNabb.

Chapter Eight

"Hey, what a surprise to see you kids here," Andy said. "Are you okay?"

"We're good, Dad, but we need to talk to you."

"Well, you look dusty but fine otherwise, I guess."

"Some really creepy stuff has been going on," Abby continued. "Can we come in?"

"Of course, of course. I've got a veggie chili going but I can throw on some more food if you want an early dinner."

"We're starved," Chase said. "Can I call my mom? If we don't show up at my house, like we're supposed to, she'll worry."

Andy doubted Chase's mom had any idea of his whereabouts. Or cared. Poor kid, he thought. No one but his paid nanny to care about him.

He started to wave them inside then noticed Johnny sitting in Lily's front yard, in near darkness, staring at Andy's house.

"Johnny Macaroon is over your house again, huh?" Dad said to Claudia.

Claudia turned around. "Yup, that's his car."

"Punch buggy yellow no punch back," Abby said, nudging her friend.

"Abby, you get his car every time. It doesn't

count," Claudia snapped.

Andy changed the subject. "What's he doing over there?"

"Sitting on a rock staring at your house," Claudia said.

"I know. I meant, I wonder why." Andy yelled across the street, "Hey, Johnny. What are you doing?"

Johnny fell off the rock and gold foil coin wrappers from Hanukkah gelt flurried to the ground around him. "Just watching the sunset."

"Mr. Macaroon, isn't the sun over there? And can't you watch from your own house?" Chase pointed in the opposite direction.

He laughed as he got up, his full six foot, seven inch frame creaking. "Oh yeah, right." He sat back down and faced the other way.

"Johnny," Claudia said. "I think the sun already went down. It's almost dark out."

"All right," he shouted. "All right. I'll try again tomorrow." He got in his car and drove away.

"Weird," Abby said.

"Yup."

"He's been around a lot lately, in your driveway," Dad said.

"My Dad's not very handy so Johnny's been helping with guy stuff. Last night he hung a picture for my mom. He could be lifting something heavy today."

If Andy didn't know Johnny better he'd wonder if something passionate lurked between Lily and him, or possibly, Saffron and him. Andy had known Johnny for years though and he never seemed to have any romantic interest in either woman. Saffron had assured Andy he was "safe." Just a friend who liked company.

Still, Andy vowed to keep an eye on him.

"Come on in kids. Might not be safe out there."

Abby looked back toward the woods and tried to focus her racing mind on one topic. Darn busy brain. Sometimes it drove her nuts, but mostly she liked the millions of thoughts in her head. They entertained her.

It was only five o'clock, but in autumn the sun set early. Darkness invaded the woods and crept toward them. The warm yellow lights in Dad's house shone through the stained glass of his windows and smoke puffed through his stone chimney. Beyond the house the scary tree waited, and Raphael—well, he could be anywhere. Abby was eager to get inside the warm, safe house. She crunched though the leaves and up the stone stairs of the brick house. "Home at last," she said. Dad led them inside.

She heard the chili bubbling on the stove. Mmm, she thought. Dad always fed them vegetarian and organic foods, but he cooked so well, no one ever complained.

"Dinner is just about ready. I made veggie chili for myself, but I'll throw some leftover mashed potatoes in the microwave and some chicken nuggets in the oven. I'll just make us a big salad and then there should be plenty of food for everyone. Why don't you kids set the table and I'll get supper. Claudia, call Lily. Ab, you can use my cell phone to call Mom. I know you kids have something to tell me and I don't want to miss a word but we should eat. It will calm you down."

After they made their calls, the kids set the giant black marble table. The chairs were made of granite. Dad bought them at an art gallery in California last fall. Beautiful but not very comfortable. For Christmas, Abby and Mom bought him some cushions and now they were much easier to sit on. Abby set down placemats for them and Chase got the plates. Claudia set down the forks and butter knives. Once they sat, and while Dad fiddled in the kitchen, Claudia made an observation.

"Your dad sure likes rocks huh? Do you think it's because he came from a rock?"

Abby looked at her, surprised. "I never thought of it before, but you're right. Marble table, granite chairs..."

"A brick house, stone steps, stone chimney..." Chase added.

"The floor is rock too," Claudia said, looking below her, tapping her foot.

Abby lifted the woven rug with her foot. "Slate."

"And the bathrooms are all marble or tile. The walkway outside is cobblestone. Why didn't we ever think this strange before?" Chase asked.

"We thought everything about my dad was strange. This stone house just fit in with his eccentric image. Now it all makes sense though." Abby whispered, watching her dad around the corner to make sure he wouldn't hear and get his feelings hurt. "I wonder if he ever realized how much stone there is in this house? Maybe he remembers a little."

Suddenly, he entered the room. "Hi, Dad," Abby said, smiling.

"Dinner is served." He set down a big bowl of chili, a platter of chicken nuggets, a salad, and a pink mound on plate.

"What's the pink stuff?" Chase asked.

"Mashed potatoes," Abby said. "What do you think?" She took a large scoop and dumped it on her plate.

"Why are they pink?" he asked.

"Ketchup," Dad said. "We put ketchup on fries, why not on mashed potatoes? I mix it in with the butter and milk to make the color more uniform."

"Uniform?" Claudia asked.

"It means make it all the same color, Claudia." Abby went to drop a little on Claudia's plate and she made a face; so she dumped a huge pile.

Abby pushed the plate toward Chase and he took a small lump. All the kids grabbed the chicken nuggets. No reluctance to grab those. Dad divided the salad into four bowls then poured his special sticky salad dressing into the bowls and handed them out. Abby and Claudia dug in, but Chase sat back. "Mr. McNabb, I don't like salad. I'm sorry."

"No, Chase? Well, you'll like this salad."

"What's the dressing on the salad?" Chase asked as he brought a mouthful of green and brown to his mouth.

"Chocolate sauce," Dad said, as he blew off a steaming spoon of vegetarian chili.

Chase curled his lip, but once he tasted the dressing, he grinned then looked into the bowl. "What else is in here? Are these what I think they are?" He held up a forkful of orange, white, and green.

Dad squinted across the table and nodded. "Yes, Chase. It looks to be candy corn, a baby carrot, spinach, and a mini marshmallow."

"I got a radish, some cantaloupe and part of a Fig Newton in my last bite," Claudia said happily.

"I told you you'd like eating dinner here, Chase," Abby said.

Chase agreed and finished his salad and his pink potatoes even before he got to his chicken nuggets. "Hey these nuggets taste different. What's in these?"

"Yeah, Dad," Abby added. "I thought everything was vegetarian here. But these are chicken."

"Soy," Dad said. "They just look and smell like chicken. Fooled ya'." He smiled and ate his chili.

Chase, Abby, and Claudia began to protest about having to eat soy, but it tasted so good they didn't complain. After they all finished their meals and drank their strawberry milk, they cleared away the dishes and got down to business.

Suddenly a shadow passed by the window and Abby got up. "Did you see that?" She ran to the window. Not a soul out there.

"What is it, Abby?"

"I thought I saw something outside." She looked out but all she saw was darkness.

Dad got up. "You know, last night while I researched Mystery Hill, my cable went out. This morning the technician said it looked like someone had yanked out the cord. Fifth time this year. Not only that, but I discovered four flat tires this morning. On my car. All the tires flattened like pancakes."

"Someone slashed your tires, Mr. McNabb?"

"No, but someone let all the air out of them. Let's go have a look." Dad and the kids put on their coats and walked outside to search for the prowler.

Johnny saw them coming and jumped behind a bush. He had to fold himself up and keep his head between his knees so he wouldn't be seen. So hard to hide such a tall and lumpy body. He feared his quick-beating heart would give him away, but no one else seemed to hear it.

"See anyone, Dad?" Abby asked.

"No, you?"

"No," she said.

"Me neither, Andy," Claudia said.

"It's such a nice night tonight, don't you think? We should sit out for a few minutes," Andy said.

No, thought Johnny. He couldn't stay in this position for too long.

"Great idea, Mr. McNabb. Aren't you cold?"

"I'm okay for right now."

Johnny rubbernecked his head around the bush, and was relieved to see them looking the other way. He slowly stretched out his long legs and listened in on their conversation.

"Here, come sit on the steps with me," Andy said to the kids. "Tell me about your mystery."

Johnny assumed they'd jump right into talking about seeing Raphael in the scarecrow tree and in the backyard, but instead they looked at each other and Abby asked, "Dad, where were you born?"

"In Bradfield, Abby." What a relief, he still believed that, Johnny thought.

"Okay," she replied. Johnny had a perfect view of them, but he remained well camouflaged. Perfect.

"How come you have so many rocks in your house, Andy?" Claudia blurted out. "You have an awful lot. How come?"

"Why are you kids asking me questions? I thought you came here to *tell* me something. But to answer the question, Claudia, well, I never thought about it. I guess I do have a lot, don't I?" He glanced back into his house, noticing everything as if for the first time.

"Have you done any research on meteorites, Mr. McNabb?" Chase asked.

"No," he replied. "Is that what this is about? Meteorites? I thought you came about something supernatural. Meteorites are just space trash. Nothing scary about them."

Ooh, close one, thought Johnny.

Abby chewed her lip then said, "Dad, do you think people can live without bodies? Like, can just their minds live?" Abby asked.

"You mean could you hook up their brains to a computer or something like in those old horror movies? Put their brains in a jar?"

"No. No, that's not what I mean. I mean no brains or bodies at all, like ghosts."

"Well sure I believe in ghosts." He got up, went into the house and came back with a book. Johnny wondered how long it would be before they all went and stayed in. He didn't mind eavesdropping, but sitting on the ground hurt his butt.

"Would I have written *McNabb's Guide to Spirits* if I didn't believe in them?"

"Have you ever seen a ghost?" Abby asked.

"Of course. I see them all the time. I couldn't write books about them if I never saw them."

"When's the last time you saw one then?" Chase asked. Johnny figured he was fishing to see if Andy had seen Raphael.

He sat quietly then asked, "When?"

"Yes, when? When did you last see one?" Chase pressed.

Dad looked around. "Right before you came over."

"Really? Did you see him hovering over there?" Claudia pointed to the back wall of the house.

Dad got up and walked to the side of his house but didn't say anything. Johnny could tell he was leery about discussing it. Saffron had criticized him for years for talking about ghosts and goblins. But Johnny also knew he would never refuse to answer a question outright, especially if it involved the paranormal.

"Not there. He sat where he always sits: Over on the back patio smoking a pipe. He's an old farmer who used to live here. Every afternoon I see him smoking a pipe and relaxing on my porch." Dad pointed. "Right out there."

The kids peered into the darkness but didn't seem to see anything. Johnny strained to see too but couldn't from his vantage point. "It took a good six months before he saw me and another half a year before we acknowledged each other. I think I scared him a little at first. I look like a ghost to him, you see. But now I wave to him each afternoon. Sometimes I sit out there and read and he just relaxes and looks on."

"Do you talk to him?"

"No, he's a ghost. He can't make any noise. We just nod hello. I did some research on the land and his name is Tom Oakley. I say 'Hello Tom,' and he nods so I'm know it's him." Dad smiled mischievously. "Want to see him?"

He flicked the light on his back porch.

Johnny grew shaky with excitement.

Dad walked onto the patio and seemed to see someone but no one else did. Johnny heard him say, "Hello, Tom."

The kids looked frightened. Johnny didn't blame them. After what they went through today with the tree and the woods and Raphael, the last thing they needed was Andy conversing with the air.

Johnny wondered if someone *was* there, someone none of them could see. Andy might have developed some special powers all these years. Hard to say.

Abby tried to bring Andy back to reality. "Dad!" He smiled and walked back to the kids.

"Dad, we don't see anyone," she said.

"No? But he's sitting right there."

Abby shook her head.

"Well, it's not important. He's there all right. I can see him."

"Well, Dad, we talked and we think that maybe ghosts," she looked at Chase and Claudia to let them know that ghosts, not Gibeons, would be the word she'd use. "We think ghosts might not just float all over, but maybe they're anchored to magnetic rocks. What do you think?"

"Hmm. Interesting theory. I don't know. Have you seen a ghost?" Andy smiled in the moonlight, excited to finally see his little girl take after him, finally believe. "Did you see one? I know you don't see Tom but did you see someone else? Are you scared?"

"Yes I saw one. No, I'm not afraid. Not really. Not anymore."

"Is he the deer man you told me about? Did you see him again?" She nodded. "And you think he's anchored to a magnetic stone?" She nodded again. "Did you two see him?" Chase and Claudia nodded.

"Well, I saw and heard him," Claudia explained.

"You *heard* him?"

"I heard him too, Dad. He talked to us."

Dad got up and started pacing and talking quickly. He shared the nervous fast talking trait with Saffron. Johnny knew when Abby became an adult she'd probably talk super fast too. "Oh dear, this is highly unusual. A talking deer man, talking, talking, a deer man. Hmm. A magnetic stone. Very strange. Strange indeed." He walked away and into his study. The children waited for him to return but he didn't.

"Dad," Abby called into the house. "Where did you go?"

He yelled back, "On the Internet. Come here will you?"

The kids walked into the house and shut the door.

No bother, Johnny thought. He'd grill Claudia all about it later. She'd fill him in. He stretched his legs as long as they could go then walked back to the field to his own house.

"The other day I read a Mystery Hill book and it said something about magnetic stones, believe it or not. And look here. It says Mystery Hill was built on a fault line," Dad leafed through a book.

"Like, it was somebody's fault?" Claudia asked.

"No, another kind of fault. Let me see how to explain this..." He tapped his finger against his chin. "Hmm. I know." Dad set the book down and then walked to the kitchen. He came back carrying a plate.

"Okay, look at this. Let's pretend a long time ago all the land on Earth was in one piece. One big Tectonic plate. Remember that word for later, T-E-C-T-O-N-I-C. It was several pieces, but let's pretend it was just one." They leaned in closer, wondering how he would explain this. Even Abby, the oldest at nine years and nine months hadn't heard of a fault line.

Dad reached over to the corner of the desk and smashed the plate. The kids jumped back and Claudia gasped. It broke into five pieces. Calmly dad explained, "So one day for whatever reason, the Earth rattled and the plate, the land, broke into pieces. They stayed near each other though, like this." He reassembled the plate. "They look like they're together but they're not really. Where the sides touch is a fault line. Get it?"

They all beamed with their new knowledge. He continued. "Okay, so if you dug under Mystery Hill you'd see it's on a fault line, that the pieces underneath aren't really connected. But they're shoved together very hard." He forced the pieces together. "With this much pressure, energy builds up and pops through. One theory states when energy is around magnetic stones and quartz crystal, special things happen. It makes people feel and see things they can't normally see or feel. It's called the Tectonic Strain Theory. I don't expect you to remember the name but it'll stick in your subconscious. This book says Mystery Hill has crystal and magnetic rock. It might explain what you saw. The combination of those things can cause delusions."

"So we just imagined we saw the ghost?" Abby asked.

"Some people would say yes. But there's another part of the theory. Or at least another way to interpret it. Whoever built the ruins might have chosen the site *because* of those components, *because* they wanted the people to see things which could only be seen under those circumstances."

"Like ghosts?" Chase asked.

"Yes, like ghosts. Maybe ghosts are all around us but at places like Mystery Hill you can see them. Maybe they wanted to be seen and so built the place."

"Or maybe they aren't all around us. Maybe they live somewhere else but the Tectonic stuff and the magnets opened a doorway for them," Abby said slowly, biting her lip as she waited for her father's reaction.

"Doorway huh?"

No one responded "Doorway?" he asked again. "The ghosts came from somewhere else?" Still no answer. "Where?"

"In the sky," Claudia said, pointing to the ceiling.

"Oh, kids. You're confusing aliens and ghosts. They are two very different entities. Ghosts are dead people and aliens are, well, beings from somewhere else. They don't need doorways. They can just fly here in ships. And ghosts are all around us. I've researched it. I'm sure."

"So ghosts are see-through dead people and aliens are green creatures with bug eyes?" Abby asked sarcastically.

"Well—" he began.

"Have you ever seen an alien, Dad?"

"Of course I have; I've seen lots of them."

"What did they look like, Mr. McNabb?" Chase asked.

He spun around in his computer chair. "They changed their appearance to look like us but deep down they were green."

"How do you know?" Claudia asked.

"They called themselves aliens and I believed them. You know I've taught you over and over again to believe. If they say they're aliens, then you have to trust they are."

Abby asked, "If they don't look different, then

how can you tell? If they're not green."

"They are green but they blend in to look just like us." Dad started sweating.

"How can you be sure though?" Abby wanted to see if he really did remember anything from his past, anything that might still be there underneath, or if he'd become human through and through. She hoped part of him remembered. It would make this so much easier.

"I can feel them. They *feel* different."

Abby smiled.

"Like fuzzy or something?" Claudia asked.

He laughed. "No, I can feel something in here." He pointed to his chest. "I feel kind of fluttery when someone near me is an alien."

"So what do you do? Ask what planet they're from?" Chase asked.

"No. No, no, no." He shook his head, "Never. If they come to me with questions I'll talk to them about other worlds, but otherwise, no. I don't want them to feel like they're not doing a good job blending in."

"So can they make themselves look like anything they want? I saw a show like that once," Chase said.

"Well, Chase. All aliens are shape shifters to some extent. Some physically change form and some just make the illusion of looking different." He picked *McNabb's Guide to Aliens* off the shelf and flipped through the pages. "They can manifest themselves as anything. Be anything," he read.

"Can they make themselves into someone's dad who really likes rocks?" Claudia asked.

"Claudia," Abby snapped.

"What did you say?" Dad asked quietly. Abby knew he had heard Claudia but didn't to want to believe the question.

"Are you an alien, Andy?" Claudia asked.

Abby and Chase froze. The room silenced except for the loud tick tock of the grandfather clock. Finally, Dad laughed. "Me?" He laughed more, but nervously. "No, I'm not an alien. You kids are worrying for nothing. Your ghost was probably an illusion after all. You had some kind of vision at Mystery Hill because of the fault line, crystal and magnetic stones. Tectonic Strain in full force. No gateway, no ghost, certainly no aliens." His hands shook and he started to look green. Not because of his alien heritage, but out of fear and wooziness.

Abby wanted to just drop it, but couldn't. She didn't want to put Dad through any of this, but she had to. She could see they were scratching the surface of the truth and couldn't help think of who might be underneath. They couldn't go back now. "But I saw Raphael in my room too, and all three of us saw him in the woods today and in your backyard."

He stood up and ran to the window. "In my backyard? Are you sure it wasn't Tom Oakley?"

"Dad, there's no one on your porch. And Mystery Hill wasn't the only place we saw our ghost," Abby said.

"At both houses and in the woods? Strange indeed." Dad plunked down hard in his computer chair and began furiously typing away at the keyboard. Chase asked him a question but Dad concentrated too hard to answer him. He was lost in his research. After a couple of minutes he said, "No. Our houses aren't on a fault line. If they were that might explain—well, no it wouldn't really—strange, strange, strange."

A knock at the door startled them. Claudia ran to get it. "It's my mom, Andy. I'm going home."

He got up and dashed into the other room. Lily Candle stood in the doorway, short and mousy. If you looked quickly, you could almost miss seeing her. But she was super nice and baked like a professional chef. "Thanks for feeding her, Andy," Lily said.

"No problem. Say, do you mind if I take her tomorrow after school? I wanted to run back to America's Stonehenge and finish our tour."

"No, that's all right, but I need her home by six for drum lessons."

"Okay. Claudia, you walk here with Abby, okay?"

"Sure, Andy. Thanks for the pink potatoes, soy chicken and candy salad."

Lily started to ask about the funny dinner but Dad waved his hand and laughed, "Oh the imagination of children. See you tomorrow, Claudia."

When they left he said, "Well, I ought to get

you kids home too." He took two books off his desk. "Abby, you read as much of this Mystery Hill book tonight as you can. And Chase, you read my ghost book." They took the books from him. "Those are your homework assignments."

"Dad, why don't you look up meteorites? Raphael said the key to everything is in the sky."

"You keep saying Raphael?. Who is he?"

"The ghost," Abby replied plainly. "His name is Raphael."

"He told you his name? Oh, highly unusual. *Highly* unusual." He scribbled down the words: Meteorite and Raphael. A green rubber alien danced on a spring at the end of his pen. It shook as Dad wrote. "My homework," he said.

"Oh, three more words, Dad." Abby took the alien pen and wrote: Boötes, Arcturus and Izar. "There, more homework."

"Strange, indeed," he said for the hundredth time. "Okay, off with you. Lots of work for all of us tonight. I don't suppose you could miss school tomorrow, to help me with this? Get an early start at Stonehenge? Chocolate chip waffles, cocoa and an early morning at Mystery Hill?"

"Dad," Abby said, rolling her eyes.

"Mr. McNabb," Chase said, shaking his head.

"Fine. Tomorrow at three o'clock sharp then. Let's go, get in the car."

They all piled into the alien car. Abby felt a buzzing on her chest and looked down to see her stone glowing. She covered it with her hand so Dad wouldn't see. When her fingers touched it,

Raphael spoke. "Don't be afraid, Abby. You're all doing very good work and there is no danger."

What do the names of the stars mean? Was Gibeon a star in the Boötes Constellation? She squeezed the stone again, but no one answered her questions. From the dark backseat she looked out the window at the bright full moon and the glowing stars. She wondered what would happen when they finally accomplished their mission, when Dad remembered where he came from. Would he miss living out there?

If the Gibeons gave him a choice, would he go back? If it meant Dad might leave, then finding the answers wasn't a good thing after all.

When they pulled in the driveway at Three Cherokee Way, she gave her dad a huge hug. "I love you, Dad."

She had tears in her eyes. "I love you too, Honey. There's no reason to get upset. We'll figure out this ghost thing. It's nothing to be sad about." He kissed her cheek and sent her on her way.

"Chase," he asked when he got back in the car. "What's wrong with Abby?"

"Um, um," he stuttered. "I don't know. Just tired, I guess."

"No, she seemed sad. I'm sure I saw tears. Why would a ghost make her sad? Isn't finding out the truth about something the very best thing? Isn't finding the answers what everyone searches for? And why did Claudia ask me if I was an alien?" He didn't hear a response from the backseat so he adjusted his mirror. Chase's eyes were closed. "Poor, tired little kid," Andy said quietly. "Oh well, I guess the answers will have to wait another day."

Chase woke up when Andy pulled in his driveway. With the doors of the two-car garage closed, He couldn't tell if his parents were home. "Thanks, Mr. McNabb. I really had a good time tonight. Thanks for including me."

"You're a great kid, Chase. I think you'll be a big help."

"Really?"

"Of course."

"See you tomorrow."

Chase smiled when he got out of the car.

Dad wove and then drove home. When he arrived, he stepped out and noticed the cobblestone path, the stone steps, and the bricks on his house. Inside, his feet touched the slate floor of his house. "She's right, lots of stone. Huh."

He couldn't wait to research the names Abby had given him. Abby finally showed an interest in his life's work, didn't think he was crazy. He'd do everything possible to help her find the answers, prove the truth was only a whisper and a belief away.

Chapter Nine

The door opened and Claudia walked in rubbing her eyes. She yawned. Too long day for a little kid.

Johnny sat on the couch next to George. A program about Wooly Mammoths played on the TV and Johnny yelled at the TV announcer for getting all of his facts wrong. Claudia and Lily joined them on the sectional sofa.

"Johnny's TV isn't working," George explained. "He didn't want to bug Saffron and Abby. He brought buffalo wings." All the neighbors were good about letting Johnny visit. They all felt bad for the lonely bachelor.

"Guess you got tired of watching the sunset," Claudia said to Johnny. She had never said anything sarcastic in her life. This sweet little girl spent way too much time with Abby.

"How was your day?" Lily asked Claudia.

Johnny's ears perked up. He was dying to know what they had all talked about inside Andy's house.

"Good. We're going back to Mystery Hill tomorrow."

He flinched when he heard the information. He sensed the kids' meetings with Andy led them closer to the truth, to finding out. He had to act before it went too far. "Everything okay over there?" He gestured toward Andy's place.

"Yup."

"You sure?" Johnny pressed.

"Why are you asking, Johnny?" Lily asked. He hooked her. She was concerned. "Do you know something?"

George hit pause on the documentary. "What are you guys talking about?"

Johnny hated to answer this way, but it was a matter of self-preservation.

"I've known Andy for awhile now. Six years or so?" Lily nodded. Claudia stared at the screen shot of the computer animated pterodactyl on the screen. "And he's certainly said a lot of crazy stuff in that time. And I know he has a history of, well, of mental illness."

"And?" Lily asked.

"And I think he's maybe lost his marbles again. You know, gone off the deep end." He twirled his finger by his head in the universal cuckoo sign.

"Really?" Lily straightened up, a pained look on her face. "Really? You think so?"

"Troubling," George added.

"I'm afraid so. He thinks there's a man out on his back porch. A ghost."

"What?" Lily's voice rose a few pitches. She sounded like a clown.

"Why don't you ask Claudia what's been going on over there, what he's been telling the kids?"

Claudia got up to go to her room. Lily grabbed her wrist gently and sat her back down.

"What kind of things has Andy been saying?"

The child tugged her hair and wrapped it around her finger. Her face turned bright red and she finally blurted out, "Nothing!"

"I hope you're telling the truth, Claudia because if Andy's sick, we have to help him," George said.

Johnny held her little hand softly and praised himself for doing such a good job acting the concerned adult.

"Yes, Claudia, please tell us," Lily prodded.

Claudia grabbed another lock of hair with her left hand and started confessing. She talked and talked and Johnny slumped lower and lower in the chair as he heard it all. It didn't seem like Andy knew much yet, but the kids did. Claudia told it all. She mentioned the ghost on the porch, and Raphael, but also brought up a host of other things Johnny hadn't been aware of. The kids knew a lot. Just a matter of time before Andy did too. He edged so close to having all the lost knowledge right in his lap. Andy even figured out the fault line. Darn! So much worse than Johnny had feared.

Claudia insisted Andy didn't remember he was a Gibeon, but it didn't make Johnny feel much better. Just a matter of days, maybe hours, before it came back to him. Raphael must have granted him memory. It was against their laws, but Andy was Raphael's son and he wanted him back.

When Claudia divulged everything she knew, Lily left the room to call Saffron. George left the room too. "I need a drink," he said as he walked through the swinging kitchen door.

The plan worked perfectly. Lily talked to Claudia, then Saffron questioned Abby, then Mrs. Sampson—Johnny didn't know her first name—interrogated Chase. Andy's credibility toppled like a house of cards.

At some point Claudia went up to bed. Johnny sat and pretended to read a Harry Potter book while the plan to stop Andy rushed along. He felt guilty for setting him up, but all he had really done was draw attention to what Andy had said. The humans would do their own damage; assume Andy had gone nuts since he defied the majority's version of truth. Not Johnny's fault. He had to stop Andy. No choice.

But that fact didn't matter much to Johnny just then, when he saw the quiet gray ambulance roll into Andy's driveway. He felt even worse a few minutes later when two attendants led Andy out in a straightjacket. From down the street, Johnny could see the frightened sad look in Andy's eyes. Tears wet his face and glistened in the moonlight. Johnny looked away quickly but the image stayed with him, tattooed forever in his memory.

Johnny was furious at himself for putting Andy and his family and friends through this, but it had to be this way. He knew exactly what would happen to Andy, because he had watched his demise so many times before from different bodies.

Andy would get to the hospital and ramble on about the truth, about a ghost named Tom Oakley. Next time, too soon for Johnny to think about without getting himself sick, his truth would include a ghost named Raphael, and Andy's former life on an exploded star. Of course they wouldn't believe him. They would force him to take medicine until he believed their truth. When he agreed with them, they'd let him go home.

Andy's confinement would give Johnny time to go to Mystery Hill and jump into a whole new body. He'd take that body and go to the other side of the world. He'd go thousands of miles from Mystery Hill, Andy, and all the fatal Gibeon gateways strewn all over New England. And he'd start a whole new life...All over again.

Johnny stopped by Saffron's house after they took Andy away. She invited him in for coffee but he refused. He just stood in the doorway watching her. "Sad, isn't it?" she said. "He was doing so well. I hope the doctors can fix him this time."

Saffron was pretty and he liked Abby, admired the kid's intelligence. Right now those smarts royally messed up his life but he had to admit it was good trait.

He'd really enjoyed the last bunch of years being in their lives, being a good friend. Wouldn't be easy when he had to leave, for all of them.

But he had left families before. It was the price he paid for living on the run. Too dangerous to get attached. He knew the risks, yet Saffron and Abby enchanted him.

He came to Bradfield in the body of Macaroon when the family bought a house in the new development. He simply wanted to keep an eye on Andy, to make sure he never remembered his past. But he had come to love both of the McNabb females, in different ways. In fifty thousand years of jumping into humans, he'd never let himself fall this far. He was truly becoming human, he thought. He struggled to decide what to do.

Leave or stay? Stay or leave? Leave or stay? Stay or leave? Leave or stay?

He screamed very loud in his head and the voice stopped. He *had* to leave. He hugged Saffron hard. When he let go and looked at her, a tear rolled down his face. "I have to go now." He walked outside. She didn't know he'd never come back. She would never know.

Tomorrow he would get a new body and the human Macaroon would return to the surface, reclaim his life. He had been there all along; thinking the being that took over was just a more courageous version of himself. The human Macaroon had been afraid of heights and small spaces. He had also been terrified of dogs. The other Macaroon was painfully shy. Johnny showed the silliness of those fears and gave him courage.

Johnny Macaroon wondered if Saffron and

Abby would even realize that the Gibeon Macaroon had left. Probably not, as long as the human Macaroon didn't turn into a coward again.

He shook his head. Saffron would never know he had been here. Only the Gibeons got hurt when they left a body.

And this would hurt all right. Johnny put his knees nearly to his chest as he squished into the little VW Bug. He took one last look at Saffron's house and mentally said goodbye.

Chapter Ten

Abby hated the whole world today. Mom asked her a ton of questions about Dad last night. She tried to lie but she couldn't. Mom told her *no*, there was not a man living on Dad's porch, Dad was *not* an alien from an exploded star, there was *no* Raphael, and there were *no* gateways to other dimensions. Mom said Dad was having a relapse, which, she explained, meant something bad happened all over again.

She fell asleep not knowing what to believe. Her stone buzzed but she took it off and put it in her alabaster box. It glowed from under the lid but she refused to pick it up.

In the morning, Abby overslept. Mom always woke her up on time but Mom was preoccupied worrying about Dad, she said, and getting her daughter out of bed slipped her mind. Abby woke up cranky. She scowled as she put her necklace on, ready to lash out at Raphael if he made so much as one peep. Lucky for him, he didn't.

Abby dreaded going to school. She wanted to spend the day under her covers, willing last night to disappear, willing time to go back to when they had never seen American's Stonehenge, when things were still normal.

Mom dropped her off at the front door,

almost an hour after class started, with a note apologizing for her tardiness. Abby handed the note to the office secretary and walked back into the hallway just as the bell rang for a change of class.

Children rushed into the hall, running to recess. Abby wanted nothing to do with recess, just looked forward to her next class and getting the day over with. She hoped, as she walked against the crowd of happy kids, that Mom hadn't been too hard on Dad. Really, what could she have done but yell at him? Well, Oleander Montague certainly answered that question for her.

"Hey, Abby McNabby!"

Abby looked up to see Oleander. The mean girl smiling with her ultra crooked teeth. She'd be wearing braces for years once she got them, Abby imagined. She hoped they pinched.

"Look everyone, it's Abby McNabby!" Oleander taunted. The crowd hushed.

"It's McNabb." *Deep breaths*, Abby told herself. *Don't let her get you upset.*

"Abby McNabby's Daddy is a fruitcake and he got dragged off to the loony bin last night by men in white coats."

After that, everything blurred. One minute, Abby dwelled on her anger, immersed herself in how much she really, really hated Oleander, even though Mom had drilled into her head that hate damaged your soul, and the next—

Abby slapped her face so hard that little Miss

Priss fell down and five red finger marks rose on her cheek. Before crazy Andy McNabb's daughter even realized what she'd done, Mr. Rossini, the school principal, pulled her away by the wrist and dragged her all the way to the office. Abby heard applauding and wondered if the kids clapped because someone finally stood up to Oleander, or because they were glad the fruitcake's daughter got hauled away.

Mr. Rossini sat across his desk and looked at Abby, waiting for an explanation for her outburst.

Finally she asked quietly, "Do you want me to say I'm sorry?"

"Are you?"

She gulped. Not supposed to lie. "Not especially. For one thing, my name is McNabb, not McNabby, and she knows it. Plus that part about my dad was a very mean thing for her to say. I didn't mean to hit her. It just happened."

"Well, Abby, a *silly* thing for her to say. You should have just laughed and said something like, 'Ha ha, Oleander but it's not true.'"

"But it *is* true. People do think he's a fruitcake."

"And was he taken away by men in white coats?" He looked doubtful but Abby couldn't say no for sure.

"I don't know. I hope not."

Mr. Rossini picked up the phone and had his secretary dial Mom's cell phone.

Abby watched Mr. Rossini's face scrunch up as he spoke with Mom. *Not a good sign.*

He hung up, his cheeks a funny shade of spotted red. "I'm sorry, Abby. I didn't know."

"Did they take him away to the loony bin?"

"Yes, it seems to be the case. But the men probably weren't really wearing white coats at all, so you see, it's not so bad. And we don't call them loony bins any more, we call them psychiatric hospitals."

Mr. Rossini took his glasses off for a minute and rubbed his eyes. Then he put the glasses back on. "All right, go back to class then. I'll have a word with Oleander. You're not in any trouble. I didn't realize the situation at home."

Before he could change his mind, Abby took the note he gave her and ran back to her classroom.

Andy sat in a comfy leather chair across a desk from a man in a very stiff suit and tie. Andy felt uncomfortable just looking at him and tugged his own loose collar.

"You've spent time with us before, Mr. McNabb," the man said, as he read over a thick medical chart.

"Yes, quite a bit I'm afraid. It's a lovely facility, really it is."

"Thank you."

"But I shouldn't be here this time. It's a misunderstanding."

"Well, that's what all the patients say."

"I guess. Honestly though, next time I actually lose my marbles, or I mean, not that I will, but if I ever do, this is the place for me. Yes sir. But I'm not crazy."

"It says here you've been talking to some children about ghosts."

"I'm a writer."

"I'm well aware of your books, Mr. McNabb."

"Then you understand. I study ghosts and aliens and, well, lots and lots of things people say are make believe."

The man arched his brow at Andy and he knew he needed to switch his approach.

"I don't see anyone bringing Stephen King into a hospital and locking him up."

"Mr. King writes fiction. Doesn't present it as truth. The same cannot be said of you as you write non-fiction."

"So you acknowledge it's non-fiction? You believe me then? That it's all true?"

"No, of course not. Do you believe it's all true?"

"Just because I write about it or talk about it, doesn't mean I believe it. Now *that* would be crazy."

"Indeed."

"So we're good then?"

"What? I don't understand what you mean."

"I've just admitted I don't believe in anything I write about and talking to my kids about research was just for fun. Entertainment. They just got carried away. I'll make sure in the future they know I'm just joking around."

"There are some pretty strong allegations

here, Mr. McNabb, and with your history—"

"History means something happened a long time ago. In the here and now, I'm fit as a fiddle. I know exactly what's real and what's not."

"Well, I guess if you put it that way, then we should let you go. Please just make sure the children you've been interacting with know this is all pretend. I think the adults involved will feel much better if you can manage to explain it as folly."

"I can do that."

The man smiled and signed the report.

"Let's get you home then. Sorry for the inconvenience."

"Oh, no bother at all. Always looking for good writing material and in a place like this there's—"

"Please, don't tell me. Why not just go to your room and get your things and I'll have someone drive you home."

Miss Sparrow was the nicest teacher in the fourth grade. Everyone agreed getting her compared to winning the lottery. Abby had lucked out and gotten assigned to room 302. With all the crazy stuff that had happened this fall, and really in her whole childhood overall, Abby knew she deserved a break, deserved a teacher like Miss Sparrow.

The bell to call everyone to the last period of the day, art class, rang. Everyone rushed out of the room. Everyone except Abby, chronically lost in thought. Did the doctors treat Dad okay? Did they make him wear a straight jacket? Were the doctors making fun of him? Were the orderlies depriving him of chocolate and forcing him to eat meat?

"Abby." Abby looked up and saw Miss Sparrow standing above her. The young teacher's eyes filled with worry. "Are you all right?"

"I think so. Yes. I am. I'm all right."

"You're a very strong little girl."

"I guess."

"You are." Miss Sparrow sat on the little chair next to Abby's. "But you shouldn't have to be, you know. Sometimes it's all right to not be so strong. You're just a child."

The way Miss Sparrow said it didn't sound like an insult. *I am just a child.* Tears sprang to Abby's eyes.

The teacher continued. "When I was little my mother had, well, she had some issues and she had to go to a hospital for a while."

"How long?"

"Long enough. And mean kids, like your Oleander, teased me all the time."

"So Miss Sparrow, you're going to tell me it made you stronger right, and you and the bully became the best of friends?" Abby hadn't meant to unleash what seemed to be her involuntary sarcasm reflex on her favorite teacher but—

"Nope. Not going to say anything of the sort. Wish I could. My Oleander, my nemesis, was a girl named Brenda. Her incessant teasing didn't make me stronger; it broke my heart. I didn't even want to come to school anymore. I had to work very hard to force myself."

"But you did."

"I did because I was strong like you. Eventually my mother got well and the teasing stopped."

"What happened to Bully Brenda?"

"She found someone new to pick on."

"I expected a happy ending for her, like she got nice?"

"No, but I didn't let her keep me down." Miss Sparrow smirked. "And after that one time I lost control and slapped her across the face, I never let her get to me again."

Abby laughed. "We're kind of alike."

"We are. I just wish someone had told me back then that I didn't have to be so strong, that it was all right to be sad about my mother. Maybe then Brenda's teasing wouldn't have mattered so much."

"Thanks, Miss Sparrow. Hey, do *you* think my dad is crazy?"

Abby's necklace buzzed but Miss Sparrow didn't seem to notice.

"Absolutely not. I have all his books." The teacher squeezed Abby's hand and smiled. "You're going to get through this just fine."

Later, Miss Sparrow wrote a note and sent Abby onto art class. When she walked in, all the kids looked up at her. She wondered if they all knew. Oleander glared at her and then grinned. Yup, everyone knew, she thought. Abby handed the teacher her note then sat down next to Chase and Claudia.

Chase wrote in his notebook then slid it to Abby. "Are you okay?" it read.

Abby wrote back. "What do *you* think?"

Luckily, only a few minutes before the bell rang, she and the others dashed from the room. Abby had never wanted to leave school so badly in her life.

At 2:45, Chase, Claudia and Abby burst out the front door with everyone else.

"Abby, look," Claudia said, as she pointed. "It's your dad's car!"

Dad's big old embarrassing alien car pulled right out in front of the school. Abby looked through the crowd to find Oleander, to say "see, you were wrong! He's here!" but she was nowhere to be found. She ran to the car. Dad rolled his window down. "You're okay!"

"Just fine, Abby. Just fine."

"Hey kids, are we still on for Stonehenge?"

Abby jumped into the backseat without question, as did Chase, but Claudia hesitated.

"Get in, Claudia!" Abby growled. "We can't just sit here in the student pick up lane. They're going to make us move."

"I'm not sure. My mom said not to—"

"It's okay," Dad said, "I talked to your mom already. Just get in and we'll pull over there so you can call her."

Claudia smiled and jumped in. True to his word, Dad pulled over to the other side of the lot.

While Claudia talked to Lily, Abby took the chance to interrogate Dad about his departure from the hospital.

"Dad, aren't you supposed to be—" Abby began.

"In the hospital again? Nope. Just for the night. They asked me a bunch of questions and I answered them and they apologized and sent me home."

He spun the crystal on his mirror and rainbows filled the car and danced off Dad's smiling face.

"But Dad, I thought, well, all the other times you had to stay for a long time. I didn't think—"

"Not this time, Abby. I'm here right? And I couldn't be here if I was still there, now could I?"

"Mr. McNabb, you didn't escape did you? Tie your sheets in knots and climb out the window, like I saw in a movie once?" Chase asked.

Claudia hung up the cell phone, apparently satisfied by her conversation with Lily.

"Dad, please tell me you didn't escape from a loony—I mean from the mental hospital," Abby said.

"Of course not. They let me out. It's not like the last time."

"So the doctors believed you about your ghost, Tom?" Claudia asked.

"No. Well, I didn't even try to get them to believe."

"But—" Abby started.

"I lied. I had no choice."

"But lying is—" Claudia said.

"I know, I know, but I had no choice. We have too much to do right now for me to spend two weeks in the hospital. I explained it to them. You kids have really good imaginations and asked about ghosts and aliens so I made up someone called Tom."

"But that's not what happened, Andy."

"Well, of course not, but the doctors believed me and let me go."

"You're not supposed to lie, Dad."

"I know. But I had to. It's a tough time for all of us. I had to make the best decision for this situation. Anyway, I'm not crazy and you kids know it. And before you ask, it's okay. I cleared everything up with your Mom. Chase, your Nanny said yes too."

"You got it, Dad. Let's go to Mystery Hill."

Abby took a deep breath and let it out. What a relief they released Dad and declared him sane. She had a good mind to march across the lot and parade Dad right into the crowd in front of Bradfield Elementary and show him to everyone. Mostly Oleander Montague if she could find her. "Look, you were wrong," she'd say. "My dad is obviously *not* crazy. He's fine. It was a mistake."

Pretty soon, the three of them and Dad would show them all. They would figure out this Gibeon/Mystery Hill thing all by themselves, send the Gibeons back and have peace and harmonicas everywhere. She giggled. Peace and harmony. They would show everyone. Whatever Oleander's

Dad did, *he* wasn't saving the world.

Johnny had an extremely difficult time getting out of his car today. For once, not because of the car's small size or his own big size. Not because his knees got stuck under the steering wheel again. This time, trepidation and angst caused the delay.

He knew once he got to the Sacrificial Stone, he'd only have a minute or two to jump into someone and then he'd have to run off. Any longer and Raphael would sense his presence and come after him even if he had to leap out and transport him himself.

He didn't want to get stuck in another uncomfortable body. Johnny wanted to be normal sized.

For hours, he watched people get out of their vehicles and walk into the gift shop. No bodies appealed to him. Time passed and he grew frustrated. Finally, though, as if by a miracle, he spotted just the right person. Too good to be true.

A navy blue VW Bug pulled up beside Johnny's and a man about twenty-five years old stepped out. Short and thin, but handsome by human standards. He already had the right car. That *never* happened. And no wedding ring. Another good sign. Johnny would have to highjack his body to another continent and that was easier to do with no wife around.

Perfect. Johnny's knees *did* get stuck under

the steering wheel this time but he freed them and got out of the car. Once he got settled into the new guy's body, he could get in and out of the Bug, the new Bug. No problem.

He followed the man to the ticket counter.

Chapter Eleven

By 3:30 Dad and the kids pulled into America's Stonehenge.

Dad zipped up his heavy coat and put on a hat and thick gloves. "It's a lot colder here than home, don't you think?" he asked. No one else thought so. He banged his hands together a couple of times and then marched the three children right to the gift shop and through to the site. He had called earlier and told the manager he planned to write a book about America's Stonehenge. The manager waved them by and refused to accept money for tickets.

"Are you okay, Dad?" Abby asked. "It's really not that cold out. It's only November."

"It’s frigid. Must be twenty degrees cooler here."

"Dad, we're only ten miles from our house. And really, it's not cold out today at all."

"You know I've always been cold," he explained to his daughter. "But here at Stonehenge, I just can't get warm. I'm bundled enough for today though, I think. Let's walk over here. I want to check something out." The kids followed him down a hill and off the site. He dug around with his foot and tapped the ground. "This is it." Then he looked up to the sky.

"What?"

"This broken rock used to be a huge monolith, a big marker for whoever built this place to see the Boötes constellation. It's the one you told me about Abby."

"Why did they want to see it?"

"I don't know. But it's the key. Boötes's stars are the key."

"Maybe they were following just one star," Claudia said.

"Maybe ... Maybe Arcturus or Izar," he said.

"What about Gibeon?" Abby asked.

Dad held his chest and started breathing funny. He coughed. "Gibeon?" he asked weakly.

"It was a star. Remember?" Abby prodded.

Dad sat down on a pile of leaves. "A star?"

"Dad, what's wrong?" Abby sat next to him. "Are you okay?"

"You said Gibeon. How did you know about Gibeon?" He trembled all over.

Chase said, "Raphael told her."

"Raphael?"

"Andy, how come you keep repeating everything?" Claudia asked.

He looked up at the kids. "I'm, well, I'm remembering some peculiar things. They don't make any sense."

All the children sat with him on the ground on the broken monolith. "What do you remember?" Abby really didn't want to know. She wanted all of this to stop right now and wished they had never, ever come to Mystery Hill in the first place.

She jumped up and ran away.

Johnny got queasy as he neared the Sacrificial Stone. The gateway within reach, right there. *So close.* One wrong step or one moment too long and he'd be captured and thrust back to Gibeon. This time they'd take away his jumping ability and he'd be stuck forever.

Gibeon wasn't a bad place. It was wonderful actually, better than any human could even comprehend. But, reasoned Johnny, being a human beat anything Gibeons could comprehend. After all this time Johnny wondered why Raphael had never taken a human body over, just to see. To try. Surely Raphael speculated about all the fuss. Just once, didn't he want to take a spin in a human, feel what the jumpers felt? If he did, he would understand better and maybe even talk to the Great One about changing the laws.

But no, not Raphael. He had so much control and so much integrity. Shucks. Johnny had to admit that he admired and missed Raphael. In many ways he missed his life on Gibeon.

The little man with the blue car walked by, just then. Johnny shook his head to clear out the Gibeon thoughts. *No, I can't go back. I just can't.*

He took a few steps closer to the man and got ready to will himself into his body.

"Abby McNabb, stop right where you are."

Abby stopped in her tracks and turned to face her father. Claudia and Chase stood behind him.

"Where do you think you're going, young lady?" he demanded.

She felt terrible...Utterly terrible. Torn between what she should do and what she wanted to do.

Here she was, summoned by a leader from another world to help her father find his way back home, where they *needed* him. And did she want to help? No. She ran off, threw a tantrum.

On the other hand, as Andy McNabb's daughter, she didn't care about any old stupid society designed to helped humans. She only cared about her society of one nine-year-old little girl who needed Dad here more than they ever could need him there. And where the heck was *there* anyway? Not even a real place, just a bunch of air.

"Abby?" Dad ran over and hugged her. "What's going on with you?"

"The constellation. You're starting to find out and I'm going to lose you."

"I don't know what you mean. What does Boötes have to do with losing me? You'll never lose me."

She glanced over to Chase and Claudia. Chase shrugged.

"Johnny," Claudia shouted and ran toward the main site.

"Hey look, it is Johnny. I wonder what he's doing here. Who's he's talking to?" Dad, Chase and Abby walked toward the big and the little man.

By the time they reached them, Claudia had wrapped her short arms around Johnny's long legs.

"I have to go," Johnny said pulling her arms off him. Tears filled his eyes.

"Are you okay, Johnny?" Abby asked.

"I'm fine. But I have to go." He started walking toward the little man again but then that man left the site. Johnny glanced back and forth and then to Abby. He wiped his eyes.

Johnny stood there studying all of them, looking utterly confused and very sad.

"Johnny, you okay?" Dad asked.

"Huh? Yeah, I'm okay. I was going to see a guy about a trip but I guess I won't go after all." He looked around nervously and then said, "I have to go home though. I have to get out of here right away."

"How come?" Claudia asked.

"Um, tummy ache. I have a tummy ache and have to run home right away and lie down."

"Oh, too bad, hope you feel better," Claudia said.

Johnny literally ran out of the park.

"That was strange don't you think?" Chase asked.

"Sure was," Abby said.

"Abby, I don't know what all this talk is about you losing me. We're just discussing stars."

The kids looked to one another. They knew once Dad began talking, he'd start remembering. All of it would flood back. And despite what Dad said, he just may have to go away.

Abby decided she needed to start being more mature about the situation.

"I'm sorry about running off. I won't do it again."

She walked over to another stone on the ground and said, "Tell me what you were going to say."

Dad shivered and zipped up his coat as high as it would go. "Up there," he pointed. "When it's dark you can see the Boötes Constellation. There's a star in it called Gibeon." He gulped. "Or used to be? Arcturus, Izar and Gibeon. Sometimes you just know stuff. I always just assumed it was really there and never thought about it. But after I read those books last night, I saw the others mentioned but not Gibeon. I kept remembering the name and expected it to be on the star charts but it's not there." He looked to Abby who patted his shoulder.

He continued. "And then you said the name, a name that had only ever been in my head. I looked up in the sky and I remembered." He gulped again. "It's where I used to live. I don't know where Gibeon is, why it's not on the star charts, but I know I used to live there. We used to look at Izar and Arcturus." He waited for everyone to start calling him crazy, or backing away from him as so many people had in his lifetime, but the children just stared.

"I'm not crazy. I know your mother thinks I am but this is real. It sounds unbelievable. How could I be from a star? I'm from *here*. But I *know*. Coming back to Mystery Hill, I can feel it."

"Dad," Abby said as she wiped her own eyes. "You're not crazy. You are from Gibeon."

"I am?"

"Gibeon used to be there," Chase explained, pointing to the sky. "It exploded four billion years ago."

"Exploded?"

Claudia looked at him. "Repeating again. It blew up, Andy," Claudia said. "It blew up and you grabbed onto a piece and floated all the way here."

"I'm an alien?" he asked. "A real-life space alien?"

"And you're not even green." Claudia said.

Johnny ran to the car. It should have been a pretty quick trip on his giraffe legs but they felt like Jell-O. It took all his strength to get to the tiny Bug and force himself in. He started the car with shaking hands and could barely catch his breath until he got about five miles away from the gateway. *Too close.*

"Dad, someone named Raphael has been helping us help you remember. He hasn't told us everything, just bits and pieces," Abby said.

"Raphael?" Hundreds of images suddenly rushed through his head. Feelings and visions...He heard countless different languages and sensed a large ball of light, a glowing orb of kindness and love. "Raphael?"

He looked at the kids and smiled, "I'm remembering. My God, I'm remembering!" He put his head in his gloved hands and sat still for a few moments... So much to comprehend. Best of all, he wasn't crazy! Never had been, never would be. "I *am* an alien! I knew it!"

"Tell us, Mr. McNabb, what do you remember?" Chase asked. All the children hovered by him.

He lifted his head and spoke. The tremor and excitement in his voice revealed his own surprise. "We split up, drifted away from the other pieces of Gibeon."

The kids nodded. Wow. They still believed him. Amazing!

"We could see Izar and Arcturus. We knew many of our beings still lived there; still do live there, in the Boötes Constellation. We couldn't get to them because they'd glided too far away. But we could feel them. See them on clear nights.

"We became trapped. Back then, no intelligent life on Earth had developed yet. We knew eventually something would be born and then we would have a purpose again."

"A purpose?" Claudia asked.

"Yes, something to do. Since the beginning of time, Gibeons have been peacemakers, helping societies of all kinds. Here on Earth, no one required our help. So we waited a long time. Eventually, fish and animals came along, but they didn't need us."

"The animals didn't need your help?" Chase asked.

Dad laughed, "No, of course not. Animals get by just fine without anyone's help. But we knew eventually some new kind of creature would be created. It happens all the time on every world: Everything is running fine and then all of a sudden a new species comes along. An intelligent species that questions all of nature's patterns, questions the order of life. They need the most help."

He looked at the children. They seemed fascinated by what he told them. Not one of them made a face at him or rolled up their eyes. *They actually accept all this. They accept me.*

He continued. "And then man was created. At first the species got on pretty well. They followed the rules of nature and the order of things, the universal laws. But eventually men learned communication. The smarter they got the more they needed guidance. We were so pleased to have someone to share our stories and history with.

"We jumped into their bodies and put thoughts in their heads, taught them about farming and about our home and the stars, taught them about the seasons on Earth. To keep them safe, we made them all wear amulets of Gibeon so we could talk to them if we needed to.

"For thousands of years, cohabitating with mankind was paradise. They worshipped the stars and planets, and Earth and the rocks, and the trees. Sometimes they worshipped gods by one or many names, but life remained peaceful. They lived in harmony with nature and with each other."

"So what happened?" Claudia asked. "Not much peace these days."

Dad shook his head. "They grew restless. Over the years they left the land of Gibeon, in Africa. They went beyond our reach and we couldn't talk to them anymore. We gave them messages in their necklaces but they didn't want to hear about peace anymore. They ripped off their amulets and left them all over the world. Discarded bits of broken peace. Once they left the areas of the big stones, we couldn't jump into them anymore. We couldn't make them stop hurting each other and couldn't bring them home." A tear rolled down his cheek and he wiped it quickly.

All the kids, even his little skeptical daughter, waited for him to tell more.

"Paradise wasn't enough anymore, they wanted all of Earth to be theirs. The time of harmony ended. First small battles arose, then large wars. Year by year they grew more violent. They forgot our ways. They started civilizations in lands far away and forgot everything we taught them about peace.

"Raphael decided we needed to help them before they destroyed each other completely. Large pieces of Gibeon would have to be sent away to where the people had gone, so we could jump into them again, make them listen. Teach them the lessons all over. So little by little we jumped into the people who lingered and told them to haul monoliths of Gibeon with them when they traveled, to place it in their new lands.

"They delivered these gateways to Egypt, Rome, Mexico, Scotland, the Skara Brae, the big Stonehenge... We planted chunks of Gibeon all over the structures, all over the world, so we could jump in and help, be a part of those civilizations. But there were so many people by then, all over the world. We did what we could, but our anchors held us fast to the stones. We couldn't help enough."

"So you gave up?" Abby asked.

"No, we didn't give up. We never gave up." His face grew serious. "I need a hot chocolate. I'm rattled."

Abby was in shock. A surprised proud kind of shock. Dad had just retold the story of the world since the beginning of time. Well, the beginning of human time anyway. He had been there for all of it. *All* of it. Heck, he lived long before humans, long before the Earth even entered the scene.

Her Dad had helped shape humans into what they were now. Had tried to lead them to living in a loving peaceful society. It hadn't worked, but he had tried. Still wanted to try. Dad and his people, or whatever they called themselves, hadn't given up.

She looked to her Dad with newfound

respect. "We're rattled too, Dad. It's okay. Let's go get some cocoa." Abby took his hand and led him along.

Abby felt the familiar buzzing on her chest. She closed her eyes and held her hands around the warm stone. "Okay." She took the necklace off and handed it to Dad. "It's a piece of Gibeon. Hold it." He took off his glove and held out his shaking hand. Abby dropped the stone into it.

Dad stopped walking and closed his eyes for a few minutes. He smiled. Some color came back to his face and then he opened his eyes. They were wet with tears. "All of you put your hands on mine." They did. Through their hands, the stone glowed brightly and warmth filled all their bodies. "We're in this together now. Raphael said if we're going to heal the world, we have a lot of work to do. Raphael has asked for your help."

"I'm in," Abby said.

"Me too," Claudia joined.

"Definitely," Chase said.

"So that's it? You know all the answers now, Dad? What do we do next?"

He patted her head. "Not so quick, little conspiracy kid. Raphael said I still have some rediscovering to do. We have more answers to find before we can be of any good to anyone."

"Did he tell you you're gonna be a soul collector?" Claudia asked

"Yes, he did."

"Mr. McNabb, how many Gibeons do you think are in human bodies?"

"Quite a few of them."

"How many, Dad?" Abby asked.

Dad handed the necklace back to Abby. "More than you can ever imagine, Ab, and most of them have no idea what they are."

"So what if they went into people, Andy," Claudia said. "What's the big deal?"

"Because the human deserves his life back." Dad said.

"The humans don't die do they?" Abby asked. *Please say no.*

"No Abby, but the person underneath sort of goes to sleep. Anyway, it's not a very nice thing to do to someone and it's against our laws."

"So is there someone still in you, Andy? Doesn't he want you to get out?" Claudia asked. "Don't you have to go back?" She made an innocent face that really aggravated the heck out of Abby. She swore her friend couldn't be that clueless and oblivious to the rules of tact. Honestly, sometimes she said things just to be a jerk.

Kind of without meaning too, Abby accidentally fell hard onto Claudia and knocked her down. "Sorry," she said.

Dad frowned at Abby as Chase helped Claudia get up.

"I don't think so," Dad said, looking at his hands as if for the first time. "Raphael said I could stay but I don't know why." He flipped his hands over and over again, studying them closely. He looked up to Abby and their eyes met.

He bordered on crying. "But there's a reason Raphael didn't just call me back home to Gibeon. We're here today. If I was going to leave my body he would have taken me back by now, I think."

Abby felt better. She didn't know if she believed it but for now, it calmed her down. Good thing too because she almost had another emotional outburst.

Johnny drove with the top down on Daisy, the name he gave his car. How the heck had Andy gotten released from the mental hospital so quickly? He should have been required to spend at least a week there!

The cold air blew through his hair. Chilly but exhilarating. The feel of air rushing past, the excitement of a car ride...He ran his hand across his leather seat and grinned. How wonderful to use a hand to feel the smooth seat. He got goose bumps just thinking of all the wonderful sensations he experienced as a human.

The smell of an orange, the exhilaration of sinking his teeth into a chilled, juicy peach, the sharp raindrops that bit into his face when he took a sip of an icy glass of ginger ale, the banging of his fingers when he ran them against a wrought iron fence...

So wonderful to be alive like this. So many things to touch, smell and taste. To see and hear too, of course. Humans had five senses, lucky bugs; five wonderful senses to perceive things.

What did Gibeons have? Nothing really. Just a sense of peace and harmony. That sufficed for most of them, but not Johnny. Not by a long shot.

A lot of Gibeons felt the same way, which is why so many of them hid in humans. It was worth breaking the law and taking over a human to be able to feel.

Raphael would never understand. Johnny had been interrupted from jumping into a new body today but he'd try again soon. He didn't care what he had to do; he refused to go back to Gibeon.

In the meantime, he may as well appreciate being Johnny Macaroon. He pulled Daisy over and bought himself three bouquets of roses in assorted colors. Before he drove away from the flower shop he spent five minutes smelling them, giddy from the sensation. He took a big whiff of the flowers and then drove to his house to eat some peanut butter and pizza. Oh, he thought, how he *loved* being a human.

"We're like air. We can't feel or touch or smell or taste anything. But being human is being alive." Andy sighed as he said it. He began to remember how it used to be, before he took over Andy McNabb.

"Our way is nice too, but this is wonderful." He smiled, just thinking about it. Even the cold sparked a pleasant sensation, a welcome feeling. He took his gloves off and swam his hands through the air, the breeze rushing past his fingers. He would miss this if he had to go, but Raphael had promised him he could stay. He felt sorry for all the Earth Gibeons who would have to return, but law was law.

He noticed the kids looking at him and he tried to remember what he had been saying. "Jumpers are trained to ignore those feelings, to get the job done and get out. But even they slip up sometimes. It's pretty overwhelming you know."

"I can't imagine living without feeling anything," Claudia said.

"Well, we do feel, but in different ways."

"But our way is better right?" Abby asked.

"Just different, Abby. Even jumpers sometimes get so caught up in perception that they forget who they are. They can't complete too many missions without getting lost."

"Makes sense," Claudia stated. "If I was a Gibeon, I'd want to stay here so I could eat M&Ms."

Abby and Chase laughed but Andy looked at her seriously. "Chocolate is one of the biggest draws, actually. That and love. Speaking of chocolate, since I'm human, I may as well enjoy it." He stood up and his knees cracked. "I've been saying this for hours but really, let's go get some hot chocolate. Raphael said we have to figure out how I got here, why *this* body, what made my experience so different from all the other Earth Gibeons. Once we understand that, he said, it will all fit into place. And then I can have my job and make everything right."

"You're my father now. Why can't you just leave it at that?" Abby snapped. "Why can't Raphael find someone else to collect souls?"

"Because, now that I know I'm not from here, I can't go back to being just a regular guy again." He paused. When had he ever been a regular guy? "Abby, I have a job to do. You kids aren't Gibeons, and Raphael asked you to help me. That's a huge honor. We have to find out the answers together and help fix the world as a team. I'll *still* be your Dad too." He could see in her eyes though that she didn't believe him.

Andy began walking toward the exit with the kids trailing behind.

"Who is this Raphael, anyway?" Abby yelled. She bordered on being called "Little-Miss-Attitude" but right now she apparently didn't care.

He stopped short and spun around. "Raphael is the leader of Gibeon. And, Little-Miss-Attitude, he is also your grandfather."

No one said another word. Abby put her necklace back on. It buzzed and lit up. "Leave me alone," she said quietly to the stone. But it kept buzzing so finally she held it.

Andy watched and wondered what Raphael was saying to her. Whatever he said, the soothing voice calmed her.

"All right"

She let go of the stone and ran to Dad and held his hand tight. "Did you say hot cocoa?" She smiled at him.

He smiled back, relieved. "Cocoa it is."

They piled into the car, wondering what discoveries lay ahead.

Johnny Macaroon squeezed out of his VW Bug. It was too small a car for his current human frame but he thought these cars adorable; one of the best parts of his existence. He had owned a VW Bug with every human body he took over since the cars came to be. When he went to a car dealer two years ago, trading in the boxy cargo van the human Macaroon drove, he forgot how large a human he had chosen. But he knew he would be stuck in that body for a while and refused to be human without a VW Bug.

Before he went home, he drove to Andy's and sat in the driveway, cringing. He wondered how much more of the mystery Andy and the kids had figured out. Johnny had been so close to escaping into that little guy with the blue bug car. So close. But then Claudia had stopped him from jumping into a new body.

He was happy to have a little more time with Saffron and Abby, but each moment he'd be looking over his shoulder. He knew he wouldn't get any sleep until he got far away from Andy and the threat of being deported. Claudia came running out of her house and down the street just then.

When she saw Johnny she waved and ran toward him. "Hiya, Johnny. How come you're in

Andy's driveway?"

"Just, um, well, so what's new with you?"

Claudia froze, her usual reaction when she hid something. Oh goodness, what mystery did Andy have up his sleeve?

"Nothing, we hung around with Abby's dad. You know, you saw us."

"At Mystery Hill, I remember."

"You said you were sick. Is your tummy ache all better? I thought you had to go home to take a nap."

Darn. He forgot he had lied about his stomach to escape Mystery Hill. "Yes, all better. Thanks. So, did you learn anything new and interesting today?"

"No." She twirled her hair.

The best way to keep safe was to find out how much Andy knew. "Say, you want to go to Carter's?" Johnny loved Carter's, his favorite place in Bradfield. So much ice cream, all homemade delicious oversized human portions, with low prices. He stood, dreaming of a Death by Chocolate sundae with extra hot fudge…

"Carter's isn't open. It's fall. They won't be open again until next May."

He deflated like a balloon. "Shucks."

"Anyway, Andy just took us to Friendly's."

"Their ice cream isn't as good." He didn't want to be outdone by the other Earth Gibeon who lived two streets away.

"But Friendly's is open and Carter's isn't. Who are those flowers for?"

He looked down at the crushed stems. His fist clenched tight. Whoops. "For me. I'll settle for Friendly's. I'll take you back there. You can get another sundae."

"That wouldn't be very healthy, Johnny. And I'll get a tummy ache. So will you."

"Shucks," he said again.

"Maybe you could come in and have a drink of water instead. It's healthier."

Johnny shrugged. "Oh, just give me a minute." He reached into his backseat to unwrap and gorge on a few marshmallow Santas. Retailers selling candy early for the holidays were awesome.

His sugar and chocolate cravings satisfied he followed the little blonde girl into the Candle home. Lily clicked away on her computer keyboard from her office down the hall.

"So, Claudia, tell me about your day. You know I love hearing your stories right?" he asked.

"Yup."

"And I always believe you."

"Yup, you do." Suddenly she brightened right up.

Yes! Again, he had her.

"At Stonehenge today, Andy remembered everything." She smiled brightly.

But Johnny did not share her joy. "Everything?" His hands started to tremble.

"Yup. He remembered that he came from Gibeon."

"Gibeon?"

"That's funny, Johnny. Andy kept repeating everything too."

Johnny ran into the kitchen and dug through the refrigerator. *Where is the chocolate syrup?* He found it and returned to the living room. He filled half the glass until the syrup ratio was higher than milk. This is a terrible mess, he thought...Terrible. He took a big gulp.

"Yeah, Gibeon was a star in the Booty Concussion."

"You mean the Boötes Constellation?"

"That's what I said."

All the chocolate on this planet wasn't going to make him feel better, and if he didn't stop eating too much soon he'd have to cover himself in butter to squeeze into his little bug car.

"What else, Claudia. What else?" he said as he hovered above her.

She cowered, frightened. *Whoops.*

"I mean, so tell me what else. I'm really interested in your adventure."

She hesitated but then continued, just as excited. "He remembered the other stars: Octopus and Racecar."

Arcturus and Izar. *This is bad with a capital...what is that letter? Well it's bad...Very bad.*

"What else," he asked quietly, hoping she'd say "Nothing" again.

"Well, then we all talked to Raphael with Abby's amulet."

"Raphael!" he bellowed and stood up.

Claudia stopped talking and looked up at him. Her wide spooked eyes looked up to him.

"I'm sorry. I used to know a Raphael a long time ago. Maybe it's the same one." He looked at her sincerely. She wasn't buying it.

"I don't think it's the same one," she said so softly he could barely hear. His head pounded and he couldn't hear much. She was such a tiny human with a tiny voice.

"I think I'd better leave." Johnny got up and left, shutting the door behind him. Lily hadn't been expecting him and probably didn't even know he'd been there.

So, Andy remembered Gibeon and Boötes, and he had spoken to Raphael. How much could be left to remember? Soon, he'd show up on Johnny's doorstep and Johnny Macaroon's Gibeon self would be sent back to the plane of bodiless existence. The world with no chocolate and no VW Bugs. No! He could not let that happen.

Chapter Twelve

The next few days stayed quiet and no one spoke of Raphael, Gibeon or Dad's mysterious life before he came to Earth. Mom apologized for thinking Dad was crazy and for sending the doctors after him. She promised not to jump to conclusions the next time.

Abby knew Dad was probably researching like a madman, but whatever he found out, he didn't tell. She figured he spent his days putting all his information together in one of his notebooks. He had dozens of them all around his place. All the books he wrote started off as notes in a pad, but she doubted there would be a *McNabb's Guide to Soul Collecting* in Border's anytime soon. All this research would have to stay a secret.

Thursday after dinner, Abby went online to read about aliens, meteorites, and Mystery Hill; but nothing new came up. She looked up the Gibeon Meteorite on the Internet and found a lot of sites. Unfortunately, none of them seemed to agree on the facts about where Gibeon came from. Certainly, none of them mentioned it coming from the Boötes Constellation.

"Whatcha reading?" Claudia popped up behind her. She was staying over till nine because Lily and George had to attend a seminar about timeshares.

"Nothing helpful, some stuff about the stars. There's about a million different myths about the constellation. One about a princess, bears, a farmer—"

"Didn't Andy say he taught people to farm?"

"Yeah, you're right. He did."

"That's probably the real story then."

"You know, sometimes, you're pretty smart."

Claudia smiled. "Come on. Johnny, the guy from this planet, wants to try out a new toy."

Abby shut the computer off and walked into the dining room. "What were you girls talking about?" Johnny asked, "Lots of quiet talking the last week or so. Big secret?"

"Abby's dad is really a space alien," Claudia blurted out. Abby cringed.

"That's interesting. What planet is he from?" Mom asked.

Abby relaxed. Of course, no one would believe Claudia. How could they? Dad had told everyone all his stories were part of a game they played. Hah! They could say whatever they wanted.

Nothing to worry about. Sometimes truth made the best defense. "He's not from a planet. He's from a star. An exploded star called Gibeon." Abby winked.

"I see," Mom said smiling. "Did he come here in a space ship?" She smirked.

Johnny laughed kind of funny as he tightened some screws on his contraption. Then he screwed one of them too tight and broke it. "Darn!"

"No, he just floated over here with his meteorite." Claudia answered.

Johnny looked up. He looked sick.

"I thought Aliens were green," Mom said. "Daddy's not green."

"What is it with aliens being green? They're not always green," Abby said, exasperated.

"No need to get upset, Abby. You know this is all pretend. But if Daddy is going to teach you fantasy, he should stick with the regular stories. Aliens are green, they travel in spaceships and they come from planets. Not stars."

"Okay, Mom. I'll tell him."

Claudia shrugged. "Saffron, Andy's not green because he just popped into a human body. Maybe on the inside he's green." That kid always had to be so helpful.

"Okay, Claudia, we know. This is a game you play with Andy. All in fun."

"It's not fun. Not really. Andy has to send all the Earth Gibeons back to where they came from and they won't want to go. There's gonna be a lot of sad Gibeons and a lot of mixed up families left behind. Abby's sad because she thinks Andy may have to go back to his real world."

"I do not! He's not leaving me. He promised!"

Abby looked at everyone. Was that out loud? "I mean, oh ha ha ha, yes, I'm afraid he's going to leave in our *game*."

Mom's smile dropped.

Uh oh...Abby made the zip-it sign to Claudia.

She decided not to say another word either.

Mom stood firm. Dad was in trouble now.

"What else has he been telling you," Mom asked. "Tell me more about the game you guys play."

"It's just a game, Mom. You know Dad has such an imagination." She threw her hands up and waved them around, "Silly Daddy, he —"

"I want to hear it from Claudia, " Mom said.

Abby wanted to jump up and down and scream, "We're just kidding around!" But they wouldn't have bought it. They didn't believe Dad was an alien but they knew the kids believed. Or at least Claudia did. Dad telling his crazy stories was one thing, but their accepting it as truth was quite another. Abby fidgeted in her chair. Maybe if she pretended to throw up... She tried very hard, but just couldn't make herself feel queasy. She got an idea. "*Ack...Urk...Gurgle, gurgle, gurgle,*" she said as she rested her head between her legs. Maybe they wouldn't notice she wasn't really vomiting.

"Abby, cut it out. I know you're not sick. Let Claudia answer the question." Mom shot her an I'm-warning-you look.

"Tell us about Andy, Claudia," Johnny said. "What else does he talk about?"

Abby wished Johnny would just go home. Why did he always hang around here anyway? Why didn't he stay home and watch his own TV? Nosy neighbor.

"Mom, didn't we already answer all these

questions the other night? And then Dad went to the doctor and told them about it being just a game? We know there's not really any ghosts or aliens or —" Abby said.

"Abby, let Claudia tell us. Does Andy really think it's a game?"

She started twirling her hair, really tight. Abby could see her scalp getting red. "Well, he, um..."

"Tell me the truth, Claudia. Does Andy believe it's a game or does he think this is all real?"

"It *is* real," she said in her loudest voice. "He *had* to lie to the doctors. He apologized but he had to lie to them because they wouldn't believe him." She started crying very hard.

Johnny stood looking kind of stunned and Mom hugged Claudia and wiped her tears. "It's okay. You know we always tell the truth in this house." Mom glared at Abby and she felt like she wanted to jump off the edge of the world. She wanted to tell the truth too, but this was important. Really important!

"He's from Gibeon and somehow he popped into the body Andy's in but we don't how. Raphael didn't tell us," Claudia said.

"Who's Raphael?" Mom asked, clenching the edge of the table.

"Abby's granddad."

Andy sat in the corner of his living room, on the floor. He wrote furiously in a notebook that had been empty two days ago but was now nearly full. So much of what he had written defied all his past studies, blurred the lines of alien life forms and spirits; but it all made sense. Made perfect sense. He still had a lot to discover, but for now he just recorded every relevant event he could remember. His first memories, his earliest memories of feeling "not quite here" occurred about the same time. He listed out many of the places he'd visited that had given him "the special feeling." He'd have to revisit those places in the future, see if they were related to this Gibeon business.

As he scrawled line after line after line, already on his second pen of the day, he smiled. The breakthrough he had always dreamt of, waited his whole life for, flowed through his fingers. Better yet, Abby was a part of it. Her little friends were being great about it too.

His phone rang and jarred him from his concentration.

Mom stormed out of the room and to the kitchen phone. Abby heard the beep beep of Dad's number being dialed. "Andy, hi, it's me. What are you telling these kids?" Abby and Claudia watched her but then she took the cordless phone, went into the bathroom, and shut the door. Mom yelled at Dad. Even through the door, the shouts banged her eardrums. Abby heard the familiar words: Crazy, mental hospital, psycho... Abby felt very sad. She knew now that Dad wasn't mentally ill. Just an alien. But Mom would never understand. Claudia reached out and held her hand. They both had tears in their eyes.

"I think I ought to go home now," Johnny said. He snuck out the back door before Abby could even say, "Good."

"I'm asking him to drive me home," Claudia said and ran out behind him.

Abby's stone buzzed. She held it then closed her eyes and listened. "I hope you're right," she said as she took it off and left it halfway up the stairs.

Just then Mom emerged, red faced, from the bathroom.

"I'm going upstairs to lay down."

Abby crossed her fingers and wished mom would look down. She did. "Why is your necklace on the ground?" Mom picked it up. "Oh." She sat down on the step. She frowned, shook her head and waved her hand in front of her face. Abby smiled. Mom saw something, or someone. "Oh. Okay, I see," she said to the air.

Raphael had told Abby he'd help Mom to understand. Looked like it worked. "I found your necklace."

"Are you okay?"

"Yeah. Why?"

"You're not mad at Daddy?"

"Oh that," she said as she handed back the pendulum. "No. Sometimes I need to be more openminded. It's not good of me to limit your creativity. Anyway, what if some of what Daddy thinks is true? If he's right and I'm wrong?

Wouldn't it be terrible if I never let you hear his side?"

"Yeah, it would."

"I think Daddy's make believe games are great for developing your creativity."

Abby didn't really like that Raphael was "helping" Mom to see the light. It frightened Abby a little bit, reminded her too much of something she'd seen in a movie about brainwashing. But Raphael didn't make her do anything bad. He just loosened Mom up a bit, lowered her mom radar. And maybe, just this once, lowering that radar was okay.

Chapter Thirteen

Friday afternoon Johnny Macaroon sat hidden in the bushes behind Andy's home. He'd parked his car one street over and had been lurking here since three in the morning. He'd been watching almost around the clock for three days. Andy hadn't left his home in all that time and Johnny wondered what the heck he was doing in there.

He looked down on the ground and sighed. Empty foil wrappers of fifteen marshmallow Santas littered the earth beneath his feet. Johnny really had to get his chocolate binging under control. Not an easy task though. As soon as Christmas finally came and went, there would be Valentine's Day and then Easter. He couldn't take a step in any direction without encountering chocolate. He wondered how some humans managed to stay so thin.

Johnny didn't want to go back to Gibeon. In the fifty thousand or so years he'd been jumping in and out of humans, he'd been addicted to them, to humanity. The pull to be human outweighed even eating chocolate, he thought. He couldn't control himself. He knew taking over human bodies clashed against the laws of the Gibeons, but was it fair? He didn't think so. He could do a lot of good as an Earth Gibeon.

He shrugged. Well, maybe not.

The problem, he realized, stemmed with him. Johnny was a faulty Gibeon. An anomaly. Wired differently than the others...And always had been, since the beginning of time.

The other Gibeons existed only to make every life form peaceful and harmonious. They lived to help, and grew their life force by creating joy. Not Johnny. He didn't care much about helping people, or any other life forms for that matter.

Billions of years ago they moved to Gibeon. But before the star, they inhabited another land. He didn't remember where. But they had always been somewhere. Always.

When they dwelled on Gibeon, when all of them lived together, they used to be able to move freely throughout the universe. But when Gibeon broke up and they got separated and trapped on their pieces of star, they lost their strength. They didn't work as well alone. They couldn't reach out to other worlds as easily. The farther they drifted from the other Gibeons, as those pieces scattered to other planes or planets, they grew weaker. For millions of years they drifted, unable to reach out to anyone, unable to do anything but hover by their pieces of home. When they finally landed on Earth, they were relieved to be somewhere where they could be of some use again.

But by then, Johnny had grown tired of helping out. He burnt out when his star did, he supposed. All those years of drifting and thinking...

Quite a long time to think about things, and when he got here and the humans eventually came about, holy cannoli; he looked forward to a change of scenery. The first time he jumped...Wow! Like nothing he had ever felt before. Different civilizations and different life forms existed in many ways, and he'd jumped into them all. But humans! Indescribable...

Forget jumping in for ten minutes then waiting a year for another assignment. No way, José, one taste of real life and he'd been an illegal jumper ever since.

He'd gotten caught before and sent back to Gibeon, but they never revoked his jumping powers. He had the gift of memory (a little hazier each day) and held the record for the best jumper they had. They'd trusted him over and over again not to stay in a person. And he betrayed them over and over. When he'd gotten caught he'd promised not to do it again. But he always did.

In last few thousand years he learned better how to elude the other Gibeons. They'd only come close to catching him twice. Both those times he just switched bodies and ran off.

Trouble was, there existed only two ways to get out of a human once you got in. One method entailed traveling to a gateway, as he attempted the other day. He'd have to drag his human form to a monolith and jump into the closest body he could find and then hightail out of there before Raphael and Andy came after him.

And the other approach to exit, he grunted, meant death. Horrible physical death. When the human body expired for whatever reason, when he couldn't make it stay alive for one more minute, he'd get booted out along with the human soul. It went wherever human souls go, but the Gibeon spirits? They went to the Triangles: horrible places created when magnetic elements, temperature, and gravity aligned in the perfect ratio.

The Triangles were swirling planes of fear and confusion. The Gibeon souls swam around the air terrified, trying to follow the humans to their next plane. When they couldn't get in, they believed they were being punished and so bounced around petrified. They howled and panicked and often leapt from the Triangles, only to arrive in a disturbing place from which there was no escape. Neither Gibeon nor Earth but an eternal hellish plane in between.

If they endured the Triangles and stayed put, the confusion would lift and they'd remember who they really used to be. They would ride through the magnetic pull of the Triangles and sail back to Gibeon where they could live in eternal peace. But those few days might as well last a thousand years for all the fear and suffering.

Johnny's gift of memory granted him awareness, but the Triangles remained an unavoidable step of his journey with each human life. Even if the time there passed quickly until he jumped into the first possible passing living body, he still had to watch the others, unable to help them, unable to make them listen. Even now he had to block his ears to shut out the memory of the sounds of their terror.

The only way to avoid the Triangles remained jumping immediately into a new human the second the old one died.

But death usually happened too quickly for a painless escape.

Sometimes he hated the bodies he inhabited or the lives he chose, but he usually stayed in them anyway because he got attached to their family or because he had a mission to complete.

Like now. He hated his physical body but had grown attached to Saffron and Abby. He also had to stay close to Andy, and Johnny Macaroon continued to be the least likely person to be noticed. He had to keep tabs on his brother.

He missed Andy very much and it killed him that he couldn't reach out and talk to him. He wanted to open up and chat about their days on the Gibeon plane and the billions of years they'd shared, all the civilizations they'd lived among.

Aw heck, Johnny thought as he unwrapped another foil Santa. "I miss you, bro." He watched the house and decided to peek in the garage. When he saw it was empty he banged his chocolate smudged fist to this forehead. "Why didn't I look in there before?"

Andy could only have escaped to one place. Stonehenge. Mystery Hill. The closest gateway to

Gibeon. Andy went there to remember. Raphael was calling him home.

Johnny had to follow Andy, had to make him understand. The Santa wrappers lay in a row, smiling at him. He smiled too then picked them up. No littering. It was one of the most important Gibeon and human laws. He headed to his car.

The Earth Gibeon drove and sighed when he thought back over his life. The Great One created him with the gift of memory. He was the only one with the gift and so became their best jumper. Unlike all the others, Johnny could go into any life form and never lose sight of his identity or purpose. Things got a little hazy but he never lost his way back. So many civilizations and so much peace, all because of him.

The Gibeon in Johnny Macaroon's body had once been Raphael's favorite son. Andy really looked up to him too. They had different names on Gibeon of course, names without words, but he didn't remember them. Hmm, this gift of memory really was fading.

Oh well, at least he never forgot his Gibeon self like the others and never lost his way back. Johnny just didn't want to go back. Human life was too precious. He wanted to be human so badly, he'd traded eternity on Gibeon for it.

But now Andy might rob him of that, steal his last chance away from him. Andy used to be a good jumper in his own right but got stuck in a human body and forgot until now.

Johnny knew Raphael would make finding

him Andy's first priority. It would be easy too, living in the same town.

Maybe Johnny *wanted* to be stopped. Maybe he *wanted* to come home. Why else linger so close to his brother, the one Earth Gibeon who could send him back?

"I'm lonely," Johnny said to the empty car. "Because I'm lonely and I miss my family." He sat in the parking lot of Mystery Hill.

Johnny felt the magnetic pull of the monolith from here, and sensed Andy close by. Normally he could feel Gibeons miles away, but he knew this time it was only a few acres separating him from a reunion with his own kind.

He started to get out of the car, tears streaming down his chubby cheeks. He banged his hand on his glasses when he tried to wipe his eyes. He swallowed hard as he took a step forward.

I can't do it! Not yet! I can't give it up. He jumped back into the Bug and put the car in reverse. Johnny Macaroon drove out as quickly as the little bug would let him.

Chapter Fourteen

Chase and Claudia stood on the large plywood box that was going to magically turn into a float for the Peace Parade next week. Well, not magically, admitted Abby. They were all going to work their butts off to paint and glue things on it. The adults helped with the heavy-duty tasks, like attaching the mechanical parts together and heaving the box onto a flatbed truck; but decorating was the sole responsibility of the kids.

Still, working on something unrelated to Gibeon for a change, brought relief. For this project, they didn't have to sneak around on Mom, deal with life or death consequences, subject themselves to life-altering events.

The gym doors swung open and Abby felt the hair on the back of her neck stand up. *Oleander.*

"Sorry, I'm late. I had to go to the orthodontist," she said.

Claudia ran over to her, stared at her mouth. "Already? I didn't think anyone got braces in fourth grade."

Oleander slapped her hand away. "No, I'm not getting braces yet. He just wanted to take a look for later."

Claudia said, "I'm going to need braces in probably seventh grade." Claudia flashed her jumbled little teeth, which made Abby smile. If nothing else, Abby had perfect straight teeth, and outshined her best friend in that aspect.

"Well, Dr. Fruiteo said I might get mine in sixth grade so by the time everyone else gets theirs on, mine will be off."

Abby rolled her eyes. More like, she'd have to wear them an extra year because they were so crooked. "Glad to hear it, Oleander. Can you come help us then?"

She strutted her way to Abby. "Oh, are you the boss now? In charge of this project?"

Miss Vinski shot a look at both girls. "Do I need to come over there?"

"No, we've got it all under control," Oleander said. "What would you like us to do?"

"Work as a team to decide the best way to express peace. If you can't come up with a group plan, there are plenty of signs to paint too. There's poster board over there."

"I'm sure we can work together, Miss Vinski," Abby said.

Miss Vinski turned around to work with the other group, and the kids worked on their own.

"How about we paint the whole bottom blue, so the float will look like an ocean," Chase suggested.

"Good idea," Claudia piped in. "And we can paint the top green so it's like Earth."

Oleander giggled. Obviously a fake laugh, thought Abby. Oleander loved gathering an audience so she could blurt out some—

"Yes, lovely," she laughed louder, loud and shrieky enough to get everyone's attention. "And let's use lots of fluorescent green so Abby's Dad's alien friends don't feel left out. Because we all know 'they're all around us!'"

That "they're all around us" line was a famous quote in one of Dad's books. It had made Abby the laughing stock of second grade when he did a big marketing campaign and had sent bumper stickers to every home in Bradfield. But he'd mailed them two years ago and no one had teased her about it in at least a year.

Everyone laughed now, even Miss Vinski, who giggled so hard, her eyes leaked and she had to wipe them. Claudia and Chase didn't laugh, because it really *wasn't funny* and because they were good friends. Also because, like Abby, they knew the aliens *were* all around them.

Abby took a deep breath, tried to calm down.

"Oleander Montague, why are you such a witch?" Abby said.

"A what? A witch?" She laughed nervously, stalling for time for a good comeback. Since Abby's talk with Miss Sparrow she resolved not to let Oleander get to her but it wasn't easy.

"Yes, a witch. You know, a mean person. Jealous and cranky and nasty."

"Oh you're so funny, Abby. I get it. You're so wrapped up in paranormal things that you think I'm a witch. Let's see, what's Chase? A werewolf?"

Abby wanted to flatten Oleander. Just knock

her into outer space. Knock her into Gibeon. Hmm, was that possible? Abby's Gibeon pendant burned against her chest in warning. *Okay, okay,* she thought*, I won't knock her into outer space even if I could. But I can't let her keep insulting me. I have to stand up for myself. And my dad.*

Oleander picked up a paintbrush and dipped it into a tub of green paint. "I really think we should paint some aliens on the float. I really, really do."

"Yeah, maybe some green paint would be a good idea," Abby said. She too picked up a brush and dipped it into the paint. Then she stepped close to Oleander. Out of the corner of her eye she saw Miss Vinski approaching, saw her mouth the word "no." But it was too late.

Abby splattered the sopping green brush all over Oleander's face and her whole front. Oleander screamed and then her teeth turned green too.

"Witches are green too, Oleander, and I think this color fits you perfectly," Abby said.

Except no one laughed this time. Well, maybe Chase and Claudia but before she could even make contact with her only allies, she felt Miss Vinski's hand on her shoulder dragging her, once again, toward Mr. Rossini's office.

Miss Sparrow and Mr. Rossini sat across from Abby in a small meeting room. Miss Sparrow looked concerned. Mr. Rossini was angry. His face blinked red, his eyes fluttered, and he clicked his pen really fast.

"What I don't understand, Abby, is why you let Oleander get to you," Mr. Rossini asked.

"Oleander can be very mean, Mr. Rossini. She's quite the bully," Miss Sparrow explained before Abby could answer.

He looked to Miss Sparrow and then back to Abby. "That may be, but Abby, she's only using words. Last time I saw you in my office you had slapped her and this time, you covered her in green paint. Her mother was very upset when I called."

"She made fun of my father again. Said we should paint aliens on the float and she made fun of my dad's bumper stickers."

Mr. Rossini sighed. "Abby, your father sort of puts himself out there, you know? He believes in a lot of things that others don't. It's okay to believe in things, but your father tries to make other people believe too. Sending bumper stickers out to everyone in town caught him a lot of attention and unfortunately that's now radiating to you."

"But Oleander doesn't have to be mean about it. That's wrong. And words are as hurtful as hands, or paint," Abby defended.

"But Abby, Oleander didn't lie did she? She pointed out that your father believes in aliens and even used his quote I understand."

Abby felt her face grow hot. "She was being sarcastic! She said all that stuff to humiliate me, again."

"I'm sure she did, but Abby, you have to stop losing your temper. Your father, I'm sure, has to deal with a lot more teasing than you do and he doesn't go around slugging people or painting them."

Abby's pendant burned against her chest. She put her fingers around it and closed her eyes. A feeling of peace filled her. Peace and understanding, even a little sadness for Oleander. "There is a reason," Raphael said into her mind.

"A reason for what?" Abby asked aloud.

"Excuse me," Mr. Rossini asked. Abby popped her eyes open.

"A reason for—I mean, yes I'll try to not let Oleander get to me."

"Are you all right, Abby?" Miss Sparrow asked.

"Yes, I'm all right now. There won't be any more problems with her I don't think."

"Well I hope not. I tried to call your father to come in but there's no answer at his house or on his cell. I did leave messages at both numbers."

"He's working on a project. He hasn't returned my calls either so don't worry if he—"

"Well if that's the case I'll call your mother," the principal said.

"I'm sure that won't be necessary," Miss Sparrow said. "I think Abby's learned her lesson."

"All right, Abby," Mr. Rossini said, "but if there's one more incident, we're going to have to suspend you. And I will need one of your parents to sign the note I'm sending home."

"I promise this will be the last time," Abby said. She just hoped if Oleander did something in the future, she would still feel this compassionate.

Andy hadn't talked to anyone in a couple of days and felt very bad about it, but strange things raced through his head. His whole body felt electrified and everything he touched sent shockwaves through him. His mind galloped a mile a minute. He'd picked up the phone a few times to check his messages and call Abby but the feeling of the phone in his hands, the sound of the dial tone—everything overwhelmed him. He didn't want to see anyone while in this state. The way he felt meant one of two things: he edged toward the verge of discovering The Truth once and for all, or his mind fell apart and the men in white coats would come to lock him up for good.

Still, he missed Abby and wanted to see her, even if he wasn't fit to talk to her. He knew this afternoon Abby planned to stay after school to work on the parade float and he hoped he could catch a glimpse of her before he returned to America's Stonehenge. He'd been spending a lot of time there the last few days, which he knew affected him.

He cruised by Abby's school as all the children left the building for the end of day release. Abby was nowhere in sight yet, but one little girl stood out front. She had screeching red hair and a green tinge. At first he thought the color reflected an illness but as he pulled the car closer, he could see an actual green tinge to her skin. Paint or dye of some kind. Poor kid. Some bully must've thrown something at her.

She leaned against the brick wall of the school, looking off toward the other entrance, waiting for a parent no doubt. Andy wanted to approach her but he didn't know her and didn't want to risk frightening her. After a couple of minutes, a beat-up car pulled into the lot. The girl tightened up, looked frightened. Andy's instinct kicked in, put him on alert. He needed to make sure the person in car didn't plan to harm her.

The car slammed to a halt and a scruffy man emerged. Andy felt his own unshaven face and imagined he looked a big disheveled as well but that was different. This man had a very angry vibe about him. He stomped toward the little girl standing by the school. Andy couldn't hear what the man said to the girl but he could tell by the mannerisms the conversation wasn't good.

Andy stepped from the car and as he closed in, he heard the name "McNabb."

Did Abby do this? As Andy approached them, they looked up.

"Excuse me, I couldn't help but overhear. Did I hear the name McNabb?"

"You're that 'crazy' aren't you?" The man huffed.

"*That* crazy? Not sure, which crazy are you talking about exactly?"

The little green redhead with a lot of freckles

laughed.

The man, who also had an alarming amount of freckles, cracked a bit of a smile too.

"The crazy who writes all that nonsense about aliens and ghosts."

"Ah yes, guilty as charged. Is that why you were saying my name just then, when I walked over?"

"No! Your daughter splashed me with green paint," the girl yelled.

"What's your name, little girl?" Andy asked.

"Oleander Montague."

"And I'm Bob. Bob Montague."

"Nice to meet both of you. I'm very sorry Abby did this to you. It's out of character for her. She's never done anything like this before."

"Yes, she has. She slapped my face last time."

"She did? I didn't know. I'm sorry. I'm sure she's very sorry too. At least I hope so."

"Me too," Bob said. "Just making ends meet and I keep getting called out of work for this."

"What do you do for work?" Andy asked.

"Was a teacher but had some problems and well, I'm not a teacher anymore."

"Dad, you don't need to explain anything to him."

"Mind your manners, Oleander. The thing is, Mr. McNabb—"

"Call me Andy."

"Andy, the thing is, I taught science. I taught the real stuff, not all this imaginary hoopla. And now here I am out of work, taking odd jobs, ready to lose our house." Oleander's face beamed red with embarrassment and Andy wanted to stop the man from saying more. But Bob seemed like he needed to say it so Andy let him continue.

"There's been some fights in our house, me getting a little hot around the collar because you make loads of dough spinning sci-fi tales and I couldn't keep a job teaching the truth about science."

"Yes, I can see how that would get you angry." Andy hated fighting, and had a natural talent, obviously from his Gibeon lineage, of getting strangers to open up to him. People on airplanes, grocery stores, trains, wherever, always felt the urge to tell Andy all their secrets. And he loved it when he turned a situation around, could make a happy ending.

"And no doubt, Oleander's heard a few of those fights—" Bob said.

"You think?" She snapped. "You and mom yell really loud. I can hear you over my IPOD even when it's so loud my ears hurt."

"I'm sorry." The father and daughter shared a look and Andy knew things were going to get better. "I really am. I guess I didn't know until now how badly this affected you."

"Children are always affected," Andy said. Oleander actually smiled at him.

"I guess you're right. I think too, Andy, that Oleander's been a bit jealous. And she's been causing some problems with your daughter. I don't condone hitting but I have a feeling Oleander has really pushed your Abby too far a number of times." *What a huge relief*, Andy thought.

"I understand. But your job? You didn't lose it because you taught the truth about science did you?"

Bob and Andy looked at each other and Bob cast his eyes down. "No, no that wasn't why. It was my own fault. Not yours at all. I messed up and was too embarrassed to go back to it."

"Well that's the first step then. I know of a man at Nextco, the community college down the road. He's been looking for someone to teach a course on how paranormal events can be explained by science. He asked me to teach it but I've got too much on my plate. You think you might be interested?"

"Of course. But I don't believe in all that—"

"You might just believe after you research it. You'd be surprised. And if you don't that's fine too. Why don't you give me your number and I'll have him give you a call?"

"That would be great. Wow, we were all wrong about you." Bob wrote his phone number on a scrap of paper and handed it over.

"And what about you, Oleander? Wouldn't you like to see your dad teaching again?" Andy asked. She nodded.

Andy reached in his pocket and pulled out two green alien pens with bouncy heads on springs. "These have my number on them. You have any more problems with Abby or anything else, you give me a call."

"I don't think we'll have any more problems," Bob said. "And thanks for the information about the job."

"I have to run to an appointment, but it was nice meeting you both," Andy said. He ran off before Abby could come out of the school and see him. He'd wanted to catch a glimpse of her but it would have to wait. Much too much to do and think about before he could see her again.

Abby walked out of the school a few minutes later to find a still green Oleander and a man who surely must be her father, based on the matching screaming red hair and freckles.

Oleander walked toward her, smiling. But not the mean, taunting grimace she usually had. This one was sincere.

"I'm sorry, I've been so mean," she said. "It won't be happening anymore."

Abby wanted to say something snarky like "yeah right," but the look in Oleander's eyes was genuine. "That's okay," she said instead. "I won't be mean anymore either."

"Okay great. See you around at school," Oleander said. She took her father's hand and walked to their car. Abby spied something sticking from her father's back pocket and did a double take. A green alien head bounced along, smiling at Abby. She smiled back. Dad had been here and had taken care of things, used his magic to help people. He was Gibeon through and through. If he could turn Oleander Montague around, there was no denying what he could do for the rest of the world. She just wished he could do it without leaving Bradfield.

Chapter Fifteen

Andy snuck through the dark woods behind America's Stonehenge. He rolled out his thick sleeping bag onto the wet leaves. He shivered, as he always did at this place, but this visit had to happen. No snow yet, a slight miracle for southern New Hampshire in late November, but he wasn't complaining. Grateful not to trudge through the white stuff.

He tugged at the fingers on the double pair of gloves he wore and pulled his ski hat farther over his ears. He fluffed his pillows, took a deep breath and looked up at the starry sky. The familiar constellation glowed above, but now, indeed, a third star blazed bright, calling out to him. He knew the star didn't exist in this time, that Gibeon had long wiped from the sky, but time ran together now for him. Memories and planets and existences.

He heard the roar of tigers, then the beautifully deafening roar of a t-rex. He heard the skitter of prehistoric cockroaches and felt the same wonder now as he had then, so many hundreds of thousands, or millions of years ago. He could see unspoiled land for miles. Brighter greens than existed anywhere now on this planet. Then utter darkness. Silence. He'd moved somewhere else. Before Earth. Another planet. The land burned red, and unfamiliar beings made desperate sounds. Creatures who needed help.

"Close your eyes, Andy, and I will show you all. You will remember all. Are you ready?" Raphael's voice boomed in his ears.

"I'm ready," Andy said. "I've been ready my whole life."

Abby, Chase and Claudia crowded around the nearly finished float. Mrs. Vinski complimented their work. Dozens of signs displaying various interpretations of peace. Children in all the grades had been painting them in their art classes for several weeks.

Oleander stood off in the corner, all alone. She'd been quiet lately, not causing any trouble. She seemed happier though, even smiled at Abby when they passed in the hall and during class.

Abby approached her. "Hi, Oleander."

She smiled. "Hi, Abby."

"Why don't you come over and paint with us? This is our last day to get it done before the parade. It'll need a few days to dry."

"I'd like to. I feel really bad for how I behaved before. I was wrong. Your dad is really awesome."

"Thanks. You met him huh?"

"Yeah, he got my dad a job and it really helped us a lot."

"He did?"

"Yup. He got him a part time job at a local

college. Then when my dad called to thank him, he talked him into applying for a full time job in the school system, at the high school where he used to work, and they hired him back!"

"That's great. I'm really glad he could help you." Abby felt such pride for her dad but also such a close bond with Oleander. She couldn't believe they had ever been enemies. "My dad used to be a teacher but quit and there was a long time between then and when he sold his first book. Money was tight and my parents fought a lot. They even got divorced."

"I didn't know that. I mean, I knew they were divorced but not that you had money problems."

"They didn't tell me about it, but they fought a lot and once I heard them say we might lose the house. I was really scared."

"I'm sorry. Wow. We should have talked a long time ago. We have a lot in common."

"Yeah, who knew? Come on, come paint with us. It's okay. No hard feelings?"

"No hard feelings."

Chapter Sixteen

The last two years with Dad had been great, and just getting better, Abby reflected as she waited for him to show up to see Bradfield's annual autumn parade. The last couple of weeks or so, she felt like she finally bonded with him. But before that, for a long time, their family consisted of only Mom and her, while Dad tried to find "the answers" to one mystery or another. Mom said the only real mystery was how he could get so lost in make-believe. "Sad," Mom always said about it. Unless she was mad. Then she said, "Crazy."

Dad traveled all over the world searching for "the truth." He missed most of her birthdays and the holidays so sent cards and presents in his place: rubies from India, jade from China, mini sphinxes from Egypt, a blanket from Northern Portugal ...didgeridoos, and rain sticks, and a hunk of sapphire from a mine in Africa ...He sent pictures of himself with the Dalai Lama, with Aborigines and Ubangis (the tribal people who put those big things in their lips) ...Postcards from every foreign place that had a post office. But he was never around for all the day-to-day stuff. Heck, he was rarely there at all. Abby banged her gloved hand on the side of the Peace float as she thought of it.

For years, Dad's fathering consisted of nothing more than a photograph, or a boxed gift from the mailman. He appeared as crinkled brown paper and foreign stamps. She was fatherless.

Only two years ago Dad finally stopped traveling and became interested in her life. He'd been much better about the routine stuff since he got back from Peru; now he acted like a real dad. But today ...Dad was nowhere to be found. No one had heard from him in days. He wasn't at his house. No calls. Nothing! No word from Raphael either. She touched the stone just in case. Nope. Cold. Raphael and Dad had *promised* that she wouldn't lose Dad in this deal but obviously that wasn't true.

Johnny showed up though. Good old Johnny. Always lurking around. He was lying on the floor of the Peace float staring up at the paper maché globe, and making sure the world would spin when the wheels of the flatbed turned.

Mom ran around taking pictures and had ordered pizza and cocoa for all the kids.

Lily had designed the float. George's company paid for all the materials and lent their truck.

But Dad? She didn't care if Dad *was* an alien. That was no excuse. He should be here!

"What's the matter, Ab?" Chase asked.

"My dad's not here."

"There's still plenty of time. He didn't forget, don't worry."

Just then Claudia walked over. "Smile,

Abby...It's a fun day." Claudia was always such a ray of sunshine. Abby managed to squeeze out a little grin.

"Abby's upset because her Dad's not here yet," Chase explained.

"Oh. Well, he's probably on the way."

"He probably forgot. He's always so caught up in his own life that he forgets all about me."

"Abby, your Dad is always around," Claudia said.

"Now, yeah, but he used to be gone all the time, even before the divorce. I'm so sick of his missions and mysteries." She wiped her eyes. Stupid tears, she hated it when she cried in public.

"Don't you think your Dad is cool?" Claudia asked. "I do. I wish my dad wrote books."

"Yeah, Abby...Your Dad has all kinds of adventures. You could make a movie just about the neat stuff he's done. My parents are boring compared to him."

"Just once, with him, I would *love* boring. Boring parents stay home with their kids and remind them to leave their teeth under the pillow for the tooth fairy and teach them to ride bikes. So I get unique presents sent to me from all over the world. Big whoop! I'd rather have him here. He promised he's done traveling, but he's not here. What if he left again? Why can't he just stay put like a real father?"

"But he's not a real father, Abby. He's an alien. He can't help it," Claudia said.

They heard a loud cough and saw Johnny spew out a piece of brownie. "Sorry," he mouthed.

Johnny comprehended that if the kids knew this much, he wouldn't be around much longer. He wiped frosting from his coat. No one had heard from Andy, which he assumed meant he had gone back. He wondered what happened to the person inside the Andy body. It was always tricky, what became of the humans underneath.

The law of the Gibeon, "no life form shall be taken for mere sport" or something along those lines, held the highest spot among their rules. There was a law *against* jumping, but jumping to give messages *was* allowed. Harming or killing was forbidden, but when a Gibeon got tracked down and sent back and left the human they inhabited, wasn't that harmful? It was to the Gibeon. How did their laws justify that?

Johnny always thought too much by Gibeon standards. He should have been created human. Well, no matter now. Once Andy arrived on his own plane and the elders retrained him, Johnny wouldn't stand much chance. If they gave Andy the gift of memory Johnny was created with, forget it. He'd be captured in a minute.

Still...he wondered what would happen to the human in Andy's body. Abby had never seen her real dad. What would he be like? Humans lived just below the surface, could see everything that happened and thought they were doing it. But that didn't mean he'd act the same. What if he had a whole different personality? Would the human Andy be even crazier than the Gibeon they had all come to know? Poor Abby. He wouldn't *want* to stick around and see that heartbreak.

Abby shook her head to get the image of Johnny spitting a brownie out of her mind. "When I was five," Abby said, knowing she was working herself up for an all out crying tantrum, but doing it anyway, "he left me for a whole year. A whole year! Even alien dads shouldn't do that."

"A whole year?" Chase asked. "Where did he go?"

Johnny moved closer but Abby ignored him.

"Peru. A whole year and the only times we heard from him at all, were when he sent me a piece of pyrite for Christmas, and crystal from Macchu Pichu for my birthday. He said he had to find out some answers about God." Abby rolled her eyes up. "In Peru of all places! Who ever heard of God in Peru?"

"Probably the people in Peru think He's there," Claudia said. "My mom said He's everywhere. Like oxygen and sky."

"Well, there aren't any Bible stories about Peru. I don't know why he picked that place. A whole year! You know what he said when he came back?" Chase and Claudia shook their heads. Johnny did too. He was standing across from them now, beside the float. "He said, 'Yup.

God's real all right.' That was it! I could have saved him the time and told him *that.* Duh."

Johnny nodded.

"At least he's around all the time now, Abby. You see him almost everyday. And now with this Gibeon thing, you're closer to him than ever," Chase said "My parents ignore me. At least he's including you. Including all of us. I'd trade dads with you in a minute."

Abby felt suddenly very guilty. She began to say something to Chase and again noticed Johnny. They needed to cut out the Gibeon talk.

"Oh, don't mind me," he said and took a new brownie from his jacket pocket and gnawed on it as he listened. Fine, Abby thought. Let him listen. What did it matter anymore?

"I'm sorry Chase. It's just that I finally got my dad back. And once he figures it all out, he'll go back. I finally got him to be an almost full time dad, and he'll go back to Gibeon." She wiped her face furiously with her glove. "What if he already went back?" Stupid wooly fabric wouldn't absorb the tears.

Johnny seemed to wonder the same thing. He stopped chewing mid-bite and waited for someone to answer.

Why was he so interested, she wondered.

"Duh, Abby," Claudia said, smiling away. "He can't go back to Gibeon. The human inside him died a long time ago. If he leaves the body it'll die."

"What?" Abby asked.

Johnny spit out more brownie when he coughed but this time no one cared.

"What do you mean the person inside is dead?" Chase asked.

"Raphael said Andy jumped into someone right after the soul left to go to Heaven, but then the body didn't die after all. But the human was already gone so Andy got to stay."

"Aha," Johnny said. "So that's it! He gets to stay. Of all the dumb luck." He kicked some dust up with his giant boot.

"Excuse me, Johnny." Abby had lost her patience. "Can we help you?"

He bit his lip. "No, um, I was just checking on you kids. Now I'll go see, um, see..."

"Mom?" Abby asked.

"Yes, that's her name. Mom. Saffron. That's who I'll go see." He nervously walked away.

"He's acting weird today," Chase said.

"What else is new?" Claudia replied.

"Wait. Back up," Abby said. "Did you say my dad jumped into a dying body? Why didn't you tell us before?"

Claudia blushed. "It just showed up in my head. I think Raphael told me but I'm not sure."

"Then how do you know it's real?" Abby asked. "And anyway, how is it Raphael is talking to you? You don't have an amulet?"

"I don't know. I was just sitting here next to you and, hey look, it's here on the float, next to me. Must have fallen off your neck."

Abby snatched it up. "I can't believe I almost

lost this." She tried to refasten it but the clasp was broken. "I'll have to have this fixed. Till then, this is staying in my pocket." As she held it, it buzzed.

Raphael's voice hummed. "It's true Abby, your father cannot leave his body. Don't worry."

"Thank you," she said, to Raphael. More wordless messages followed which she relayed to her friends.

"My dad has to stay here now or else his body will die. He couldn't go anywhere even if he wanted."

Abby hugged Claudia. Dad wasn't going anywhere. "What about his soul though? How did Dad find a dying body? Did someone happen to drop dead there on Mystery Hill?"

"I don't know," Claudia said. The amulet was silent too.

"Do all the Earth Gibeons go into dead bodies?" Chase asked.

Claudia shrugged again.

"How could they?" Abby said. "When somebody dies, they die. Their body says 'I've had enough' and that's that. It must have been a special situation." She held her stone and quietly asked Raphael. The kids watched her but nothing happened.

"Hey, food," Claudia yelled. They looked up and saw that the pizza guy had dropped off their lunch. They each ran and gorged themselves on pizza and cups of steaming cocoa.

Abby looked up to see Mimi and Grampy

walking toward her. They were Dad's parents. "Maybe they have some answers," Abby said through a mouthful of cheese.

Mimi gave Abby a big hug. Grampy leaned over and kissed her cheek. "I'm so proud of your float. You guys did a great job. Did you do all the pictures covering the float?"

"Yup. Well, all the kids in the school," Abby said. "We were supposed to draw world peace. Some kids' pictures are on sticks too that the parents can carry. Mom, Johnny, Lily and George are carrying sticks."

"What about your father?" Grampy asked. He thought Dad was a "certifiable fruit loop," whatever that meant. He wanted Dad to have a real job to go to everyday instead of chasing around the globe and writing about "stuff and nonsense."

"He's coming," Abby said, hoping that was true. "He's going to see us off then drive to where the parade ends to pick us up."

"So where is he then?" Grampy looked to Mimi. "Where is he, Judi? Off chasing little green men? For the life of me, I don't know what's wrong with that kid." He banged his cane on the ground.

"Andy," Mimi said sternly. Grampy's name was Andy too. Abby would have been Andrew Peter McNabb III but she ended up being a girl. "He's not a kid anymore. He's thirty-eight," Mimi replied.

"Even more reason to be on time for things.

Abby, get me some hot chocolate will you, please?" Abby ran off.

Abby brought back the cup and gave it to her grandfather just as Claudia asked, "Mrs. McNabb, did you ever go to America's Stonehenge?"

Mimi stiffened up.

"I went twice," she said. "But there's nothing to tell. I think it's time for the parade to start. We should go find a place to stand."

"It's not time yet. It's 12:38 so we have, hold on." She whispered to Abby, "What's thirty-eight take away one o'clock?" Abby whispered the answer. "We've still got twenty-two minutes left," Claudia announced.

"It's not a great story. Not interesting at all."

"Please, Mimi," Abby asked.

"All right then. I went to Mystery Hill with Grampy one day. We wandered around and followed the map just like all the other tourists. When I left, I heard a voice tell me to come back. It didn't say when, just that I had to come back. It was so strange. I looked around but didn't see anyone, so Grampy and I went home."

"Huh. You heard a voice tell you what to do? That is weird," Chase said, shooting looks to Abby and Claudia.

"I figured it was just my imagination because you know Grampy and I don't believe in all that mumbo jumbo. But it just wouldn't get out of my head."

Claudia began to speak but Abby jabbed her hard.

Mimi continued. "Back then, when your dad was little, I worked for the governor. I was one of his assistants. Months after I visited Mystery Hill, we had planned a big luncheon for the governor. Lots of other politicians were coming to discuss what to do about the Vietnam War. It was a very important meeting and I should have been excited about the luncheon. President Lyndon B. Johnson was planning to attend.

"But I couldn't get that voice out of my head, the one telling me to come back to Mystery Hill. It's not as if I still heard the voice, but I remembered it. I couldn't get my mind off of it."

Mimi started to look upset suddenly. Johnny flinched and took a few steps back.

Wasn't he supposed to be looking for Mom? Abby wondered.

Grampy touched her arm again. "Judi, you don't have to talk about it. What good will it do?"

She shooed him away. "And what harm will it do? Abby has the right to know about the day her father almost died."

"Died?" Abby asked. Her eyes popped open like checkers and she started to feel queasy. So that's when it happened. When Dad was only a little kid.

Claudia squeezed her hand tight to comfort her. "But he didn't die, right, Mimi?" Claudia asked.

"Of course he didn't," Chase explained. "He's here isn't he? He grew up and got married and had Abby."

"Duh. That was the other Andy." Claudia made a face at Chase and he nodded.

"What other Andy?" Mimi asked.

"Never mind her. She gets confused. Tell us about that day," Abby implored.

By now, Johnny seemed to have forgotten all about Mom and was standing beside Mimi. Abby didn't blame him really. It was a compelling story.

"I need to sit down over here on this rock." Mimi said. "It was the day before the luncheon. It was snowing something fierce. Grampy went to church but your dad had a cold so we stayed home. That message in my head had gotten so strong I couldn't stand it anymore. I had to go, right then, so I finally bundled little Andy up. Back then families didn't have two cars so I called a taxi. It's crazy, now that I think about it. Calling a taxi in a snowstorm to drive me all the way out there but I had to.

We swerved all the way there and the driver kept asking me if I was sure I wanted to go. I told him I'd never been surer of anything in my life. We finally got there and it was closed. Now it's open year round I think, but back then—well anyway, I didn't even care. The taxi driver thought I was nuts but he escorted me anyway as I walked right onto the site."

"Your Mimi broke the law," Grampy said. "Isn't that a hoot?"

"I didn't mean any harm, just needed to be there. The driver said he didn't want to leave me alone. I walked around the site as I had before, waiting for something to happen. To find out what the heck I was doing there. But nothing happened. Your dad wriggled like crazy so I set him down by one of those rock walls.

"I saw an interesting rock on the ground and picked it up. Even though it had been sitting in the snow, it was warm. I remember it felt warm." A peaceful smile covered her face.

"Judi," Grampy nudged her with his cane.

"Well, yes, where was I? I was holding the stone and thinking that the governor would like it...That I should give it to him before the luncheon. That it would be like a good luck charm to him. I had to give it to him. It's all I could think about. Next thing, I looked down and Andy was gone. He had wandered off in the snow. The driver had headed to the exit, was getting nervous we'd get in trouble for trespassing. I screamed your dad's name over and over. I ran around and slid on some ice but I got up." She rubbed her wrist as if she could still feel where she had banged it so many years ago. "The driver heard me and came running back and we both called out, but we just couldn't find him. No cell phones back then either. I went crazy, racing all around the site, inside the ruins. The driver rushed back to his cab to use his radio to call the police."

"You okay, Judi?" Grampy asked.

"I'm fine. It's time Abby heard this story. While we waited for the police, the driver and I searched and searched. It was snowing so hard by then that it I couldn't see a foot in front of us. It was early November then, too early for that much snow, but you know New England."

Claudia grabbed Johnny's hand and their mouths both dropped open. Abby and Chase were eager to hear the part when Andy would be saved. Poor Mimi, she thought.

"Then all of a sudden, there he was." Mimi wiped a tear from her eye. "He was laying right there on the Sacrificial Stone, of all places. We ran all over the place and he was there the whole time. But he was frozen and not breathing. I picked him up and hugged him, wrapped him in my coat and ran back to the parking lot. Because of the snowstorm, the police still hadn't made it there so I jumped in the back of the cab and we took off."

Mimi's hands shook but she kept talking.

"Little Andy wasn't moving. He had no heartbeat. I just kept crying. And the whole time I was holding that silly, stupid rock. If it hadn't been for that rock, I never would've lost him."

"But then he was fine, Judi." Grampy hugged her. "You don't have to drag out the story. He was fine."

She nodded. "He was fine. I really thought he was gone forever but on the way to the hospital his eyes opened. He looked confused and scared, like he had never seen me before, like he had never seen anything before. He started crying like a newborn baby, like he was seeing the world for the first time and was scared as heck. I could feel the rock getting even warmer in my hand, crazy as that sounds, so I let him hold onto it. After that, he calmed right down.

"We took him to the doctor but they said he was fine. After that, for years, that silly rock was like a security blanket. He carried it everywhere."

Abby, Chase and Claudia looked at each other. Now it all made sense. That rock was supposed to go to the governor so the Gibeons could talk to him, give him a peace message; but tragedy got in the way. Abby's dad really had died. And the man who had raised her was an alien. Huh.

"So the governor never got the rock did he?" Claudia asked.

"No, I guess he didn't. After that, I never thought about giving it to him again. I had no urge to ever go back to Mystery Hill. So that was that. End of story."

Hardly the end of the story, Abby thought.

"Whatever happened to my Dad's rock?"

"I'll tell you what happened to it," Grampy said. "I got rid of it once and for all. Your father had all this crazy talk. He was a wacky little kid, always talking about his other home and his other family. Nuts." He tapped his cane to the side of his head.

"Mimi took him to a doctor when he was about nine or ten and they said he just had a good imagination. All I know is that he was acting crazy and it was all because of that stupid little rock. One weekend we went camping in

Bridgewater by the Hockomock Swamp, and I threw it out into the woods. After that, Andy was fine."

The principal called them over to the float. "We have to go," Abby said. "See you on Main Street."

The kids all jumped onto the float and grabbed the paintings they'd be holding up.

"They threw his rock away. No wonder he couldn't remember anything," Chase said, balancing on his knees in the float and facing his mother's camera.

"But he kind of remembered. That's why he's crazy right?" Claudia asked. She faced toward Lily. The flash whitened her face.

"Everyone, keep smiling," Lily Candle called out.

They smiled and balanced and held their pictures. But they managed to talk too. "Yeah, that's why. Grampy shouldn't have thrown the rock away," Abby said.

"So the whole thing was just an accident. He was in Mimi for just a minute to make her bring the rock to the governor and next thing he was in a little boy's body with no idea where he was," Chase said.

"They were in the car and far away from the gateway when he jumped from Mimi into my Dad. Maybe in emergencies like that they can jump with just the necklace."

"No," Claudia said. "They have to be near a gateway. He jumped from your Mimi to your dad when he was frozen on the Sacrificial Table. He was needed more inside the boy so he jumped in there. He didn't plan on staying, just helping out to get the other little boy to come back. But he didn't come back and then Mimi and him ran off the site and drove away. That's how he got stuck."

"I see," Johnny said.

Where did *he* come from? Abby wondered why he wouldn't bug off.

Claudia looked at him curiously. "Now I get it," Johnny said. They all looked up to his big figure, wondering why he was still there.

"Get what?" Abby asked. She accepted Johnny wouldn't go away and he did seem interested. None of the other adults were.

"Never mind." he walked away.

Abby shook her head. Weird man. "Hey, I bet that's why my Dad's always cold."

"Why?" Claudia asked.

Abby threw down her painting. "His first memory was in a body that almost froze to death!"

Claudia threw her picture down too. "And he got even colder at Mystery Hill, remember?"

As the float started to pull away, and Abby and Claudia picked up their pictures, they heard the screech of car wheels.

Dad's alien car sped through the emptying field. Grampy and Mimi looked at it and Abby could tell Grampy was ready to say, "What's wrong with that kid?" when Dad stopped the car and got out. He ran over to the float, oblivious to his parents or any of the other people that were frowning because he parked in a walking area. Or the fact that the parade had started and no one but sign carriers could be there.

"Daddy," Abby yelled, throwing her picture down again and waving. "You're back."

He ran beside the float as it moved and the giant paper maché Earth spun. "I figured it out, kids. I figured it out!" He was smiling so hard, Abby was sure his mouth must be sore.

She noticed that Johnny had backed away. He looked sad for some reason. Why did he even care about all of this? He must be one of those adults who believed in all the stuff Mom said was pretend. The ones who bought Dad's books. But why should Johnny be sad about it? Weren't people like him always looking for the answers? Maybe he felt left out.

Dad poured out his story like water from a fire hose. "I went back to Mystery Hill and camped out for a couple of days. I hid in the woods alone but I finally remembered. You won't believe it." He walked beside the float.

"Yes, we will, Mr. McNabb. We talked to your mom and she told us everything," Chase said. He nodded toward Mimi and Grampy.

Dad turned around and saw his parents. Grampy frowned at him. "Really? They know I'm an alien?"

"Alien? Jiminy Crickets," Grampy shouted. "What's wrong with that kid?" He banged his cane hard on the ground.

"He's not a kid, Andy. He's thirty-eight," Mimi reminded him.

Andy laughed. "Whoops. Guess they didn't know that." The kids laughed too.

"They didn't figure it out. We did," Claudia said.

"We know why you got in that body," Abby yelled.

He nodded and grabbed a sign so he could run alongside them. "Isn't it great though? I almost ended the whole Vietnam War."

Ended the Vietnam War? They hadn't figured that part out, thought Abby. Wow. Chase and Claudia had their wow faces on too.

"If I hadn't jumped into that kid, into me, I would have changed the world. And now that I can remember it all, who knows the great things we can do!" He jumped up and down. "Here's to peace!"

She saw Dad and Johnny catch each other's eyes. He waved to Johnny and shouted, "Here's to peace!"

Johnny smiled and joined him in the march. "Here's to peace," he mouthed.

"Here's to peace," the three kids shouted. All the children on the whole float shouted it too, thinking it was part of the parade show. "Here's to peace. Here's to peace!" Finally the adults started chanting it too.

Holding a sign and walking beside the float with the others, he quietly said, "Here's to peace," as he winked at Abby. People on the street smiled when the Peace float went by and Abby could see how much good her Dad really could do; how much good they could all do together to make the world a better place.

As the float moved, the world spun round and round and the children, the adults, and her alien Dad shouted for peace.

Chapter Seventeen

Johnny's human birthday fell on a Saturday and Lily, George and Claudia invited him over for a party. He really liked the human tradition of getting presents and cake. His favorite part of the day though was blowing out the candles and making a wish. He wished for the same thing in every body he ever had: to be human for just one more year. Of course he never wished that out loud.

Johnny rolled into the driveway around noon knowing that Saffron and Abby would also be there. That brought him joy, but also mixed feelings about Andy. Who knew what would happen if he showed up? He smiled when he saw the blue balloons on Lily's mailbox. He loved how the Candles and McNabbs had accepted them into their families, treated him like one of their own. As he squeezed out of the Bug, and dreamed about what kind of cake they got—*please let it be ice cream cake with crunchies and a picture of me on top*—a delivery truck passed and drove to Andy's house.

Suddenly, Johnny felt nauseated and dizzy. He leaned against the car and took deep breaths. He glanced down the street as a short pudgy guy in shorts and a tall skinny guy also in shorts rolled a big box out of the back. Johnny never understood why deliverymen wore shorts even in fall and winter, but he thought maybe they got hot moving all those boxes. He rested his head on his hands and watched. Their faces looked strained even though they were using a tow dolly to roll the package along. Must be really heavy, he thought. Must be a new refrigerator.

He felt sick all of a sudden. He walked into the house hoping he wasn't catching the flu. Being sick on your birthday was no fun at all.

A couple of hours later, Johnny felt much better. He had opened all of his presents, stuffed himself full of ravioli and garlic bread and was on his second piece of ice cream cake. He had made his usual wish to be human and blew out every last candle on the first try. After that he was relieved. He would get another year after all. Maybe Andy wouldn't make him go back. Maybe Johnny had blended in so well that Andy wouldn't be able to spot him, even right under his nose. He looked down at his hands. Maybe he had turned into a human and didn't even know it!

Johnny looked over at Andy. Here he was sitting right across from his Gibeon brother and he hadn't even hinted that he recognized him. Or maybe he did but Raphael had said he'd allow Johnny to stay.

If that were the case, he wasn't going to rush back to Mystery Hill and into some stranger. No way.

If Andy didn't say anything to him by the end of November, he'd know he was safe. Johnny took another bite of cake and grinned. What a wonderful life he had.

Andy sat across from Johnny. Sad. Terribly, horribly sad. He adored his older brother, always had, and always would. But he broke the law of the Gibeons over and over again and their father said Johnny had to come back. Raphael instructed Andy to just keep an eye on him until it was time for transport. He was supposed to continue to pretend he didn't know that Johnny was a Gibeon. But of course he did. He knew it at the parade when he had returned from camping out at Mystery Hill. Raphael granted him full memory so he could collect all the lost souls.

When Andy got to the parade, Johnny was so easy to spot. It wasn't that he looked any different but suddenly Andy could feel him. Andy had smiled at him, so glad to finally see him again for what he was. He wanted to jump over and give him a human hug, but he couldn't. Raphael had been very specific. He was not to divulge that he recognized him as a Gibeon.

Seeing him here now, so happy, he was tempted to beg Raphael again to let him stay. The kids were so attached to this Johnny Macaroon. What if the one underneath was a jerk? He had already suggested that Johnny be allowed to keep his human form and become a soul collector too, but Raphael had refused.

Johnny Macaroon would return to Gibeon and his jumping powers would be revoked.

There was no punishment on Gibeon, not like on Earth. There was no pain or anger or loneliness. Raphael's restraining him was not for the sake of punishment, but for relearning the Gibeon ways. Once Johnny redeemed himself and became pure again, devoted to helping the other life forms, he could jump again. But that could take thousands of Earth years.

Andy knew that far in the future, humans and the planet Earth might be long gone. Sad. Very sad.

But it was not Andy's place to contradict or question what Raphael wanted. He had a job to do. He was a soul collector and Johnny Macaroon was housing a Gibeon soul. He'd give him a little longer. Once the new gateway was completed though, Johnny would be the first to go back.

Chapter Eighteen

Everyone celebrated Thanksgiving at Abby's house. The Candles and Dad came too. And of course Johnny. Abby couldn't shake that guy. Mom said Johnny had nowhere else to go and she didn't want him alone on a holiday. Mimi and Grampy were in Florida on vacation and Mom's parents, well, they lived pretty far away and Abby didn't see them very often.

They had all the regular foods: turkey, stuffing, sweet potatoes, corn... and Lily brought pumpkin lasagna the kids didn't like at all but the adults loved. Johnny brought a three layer chocolate cake and Dad brought a pecan pie, homemade chocolate pudding, and a tofu version of turkey with vegetable broth gravy. It tasted funny until he poured maple syrup all over it.

After dinner Dad gave a speech, giving thanks, grateful to have such a nice and supportive family. Saffron smiled and squeezed his hand. "We're glad to have you too, Andy."

"Saffron, you've done a great job raising Abby. I'm sorry I wasn't around for more of it."

"Well, you're here now."

"That's the thing," he started.

Abby perked her head up. *What was he saying?* She touched her amulet that hung around her neck on a new chain, but it was silent.

"I have some stuff I have to do."

Unbelievable.

"Stuff I have to do," was Dad's euphemism for "I have to disappear for awhile."

"Are you leaving?" Abby asked. Tears sprang to her eyes.

"Yeah, Andy. Are you leaving?" Johnny asked. The chubby guy with glasses was really starting to get on Abby's nerves. He was always so interested in what the kids were doing. *It was none of his business!* She took a deep breath to relax and hoped her face hadn't turned as bright red as it felt.

Andy just answered to his daughter.

"Abby, I can never leave. You must know that by now. But I can't do everything I need to do from here. There's a greater good."

"Greater good? I'm the greater good. What's more important than me?" she fumed.

"The rest of the world...Duh, Abby," Claudia said. Dad nodded.

Mom rolled her eyes up. "Lily, want to help me get the desserts?"

Lily nodded and stood up. George followed. "I'll help too."

George wasn't good in social situations. He hardly ever talked at all and he never spoke to Abby except to say, "Hi." He was lost whenever he tried to have a conversation with Dad. Of course he confused a lot of people because sometimes his conversations were a little tough to follow, but he seemed to make George Candle especially uncomfortable.

Once the other grownups left the room, Claudia pointed to Abby's neck. "Anyway, wherever he goes, he can always talk to you in your necklace. Right, Andy?"

"That's right, Claudia."

There were so many reasons Andy wished he had never found out this true beginnings as a Gibeon. It would make his life hard and he'd have to leave his daughter for long periods of time. It would be easier now with her pendant and they could communicate, but physically he wouldn't be around to watch her grow up. Heartbreaking for him and for her too, he was sure.

But in other ways, Andy was relieved that he was a Gibeon. It explained why he had spent his whole life feeling out of place, detached. He had always felt he had a grand world-changing mission he was supposed to complete. Enlightening folks on the paranormal with his books just wasn't fulfilling. Now he knew. He really was important and needed; and despite what his Earth father told him all the time, he wasn't crazy.

As much as he'd love to stay here with Abby, doing all the routine stuff, he had to travel around the world and round up the Gibeons.

He looked over at Johnny and had never seen him happier. And "never" was a long time considering it included the beginning of eternity.

It utterly crushed Andy to see him so happy and know that he had to take it all away. Absolutely crushed him that he had to send him back. But there was no other way. He had begged and pleaded with Raphael but Johnny definitely had to go back. Raphael stressed over and over again the law that prohibited the taking over of human lives.

There was a human Macaroon underneath and Andy admitted it was only fair he be allowed to have his life back, but he was miserable about having to send his brother home. Johnny would never forgive him. Andy would never forgive himself. He shook his head. No. That wasn't true. Humans didn't forgive but Gibeons did. They didn't have resentment on their plane.

The Gibeon in Johnny Macaroon's body would be sad, but once he got back home, all would be forgotten and he'd be thrilled to be back. At least Andy hoped so.

He stared off into space thinking about all of it. He heard a loud snap and looked up.

"Andy!" Saffron snapped her fingers under his nose. "Pay attention. No drifting off into your other worlds at dinner time," she said, flashing him an I'm-just-teasing glance.

"Didn't even hear you guys come back in the room." Lily, George and Saffron were sitting at the table and had set out the desserts and coffee. Andy shook his had to try and propel himself back in the here and now. He grinned. "Ooh, sweets." He helped himself to a slice of Johnny's chocolate cake and his own chocolate pecan pie.

Claudia tugged his arm. "So like I said, I thought we were going to help you on your missions, Andy."

"Help you how?" Saffron asked.

All the other adults looked at him, awaiting an answer. To Saffron he answered, "Since I have to go away, I thought this time if I involved Abby, she might not feel so...alienated. No pun intended."

"Involved how?"

"Research mostly." Saffron would be happier hearing that.

"And I'm helping too. And Chase," Claudia said. "Right?"

"That's right. The kids have been instrumental in something I've been working on recently. There are some missions I could really use some help with. I know this stuff isn't real and so do they but this is my job. It'll be good experience for them." That was about the biggest lie he'd ever told.

Johnny cleared his throat.

Abby wondered if he was going to ask if he could help too.

"What kind if missions exactly?" Lily asked. "I don't want Claudia traipsing all round the country looking for ghosts."

"Or around the world," Saffron said. "Local mysteries only...And nothing too bizarre."

Dad shrugged as if to say, "You think

everything's too bizarre, Saffron." but he didn't. Instead he just said, "There are plenty of local mysteries."

"Where are you going? What are you up to now?" Saffron asked. Abby knew Mom hated his habitual running off as much as she did.

"World peace...actually," he smiled at the girls.

"World peace. Really?" Saffron frowned. "I'll believe that when I see it."

"Oh you'll see it. Right kids?" Claudia nodded and Abby just stared. She knew she was being selfish. The rest of the world needed her Dad and them to make it right. Yet she contemplated ways to hold him back. She touched her necklace. Dad could always talk to her wherever he went, she reasoned.

Even though Mom still thought he was crazy, he might just drive the world to peace after all. Maybe he could do it. Maybe they could do it together. Mom didn't believe it, but she didn't even believe in Santa either.

Abby looked over at Mom, who threw her hands up. "We'll be here when you get back, Andy. We always are."

"Where are you going first?" Johnny asked. Nosy old Johnny.

"Back to where it all started, I guess. South Africa."

"South Africa?" Johnny asked. His chubby hands started to shake.

Andy nodded.

"Where what all started?" Mom asked.

Dad didn't answer. He knew how easily Mom got riled. The kids knew too so no one answered her question. She waited but all was silent. "Where *what* all started?"

Claudia told the truth, knowing no one would believe it anyway. "It's where Andy's star crashed and where the first Earth Gibeons were made."

"I see. Okay then," Mom said. She smiled and mouthed the words "their little game" to Lily. She got up to clear the dessert plates. Lily followed suit. So did George who had been gradually moving farther and farther away from Dad all through dessert.

"I gotta pee," Johnny said. Then he blushed. "I mean, use the men's room." He got up too.

"So, my little conspiracy kids," Dad said once all the adults had left, "I need you to take care of things while I'm away. Achieving world peace is not a one-man job."

"Or a one-alien job," Claudia said.

Abby shot her a look. "Okay, that's enough about the alien stuff." To Dad she asked, "Can we do it without you being here?"

"Of course. Raphael said—" Johnny walked back in the room so Dad stopped quick. "Say, why don't you kids come to my house for a few minutes and I'll explain everything? Run in the kitchen and ask your moms."

Abby and Claudia went to ask. Luckily Mom and Lily both said okay. George Candle nodded. Mom peeked her head back into the dining room.

"I'm happy you're including Abby in your work but nothing otherworldly okay?"

"Sure."

"No rides on stars or anything." She winked at Andy.

"We can't ride stars, Saffron. We're human. Only Andy can," Claudia said.

Lily raised her eyebrow.

Dad patted Claudia on the head. "Yup, I ride stars all the time. What a creative little girl you've got here."

"Okay, whatever. Have fun guys," Lily said. She disappeared back into the kitchen.

When Abby and Claudia got into the car, Dad said, "We need Chase too. It has to be all three of you. It's what Raphael wants. Abby, here's my cell phone. Call him and see if he can come over for a few minutes."

"Sure Dad." While Abby dialed, Andy drove the car to Chase's house, about two minutes away. They were in his driveway by the time Chase said "Hello."

"Chase, we're in the driveway. You need to come over my dad's house right away. He said he has to show us something and we have to take over his mystery business while he's away."

Chase stepped out the front door, still holding the phone. He hung up the phone and approached the car.

"Hi. What's up?"

"Can you come over for a little while, Chase? I know it's a holiday, and family time but—" Dad asked.

"That's okay. We went out to the Bradfield Yacht Club for a Thanksgiving buffet hours ago. Now my parents are just in there reading. We were going to watch a movie but I'm sure they won't care."

"I'm sure they'll care. They won't *mind*," Dad said. He always liked to think the best of people. Abby knew Chase's parents pretty well though and honestly, all they did seem to care about were their careers.

"Let me go ask them," Chase said. "Be right back."

Within seconds he returned with his jacket on. He sat in the back and whispered to Abby, "They don't care."

She squeezed his hand. "We care."

Abby was glad Chase joined them in this Gibeon business. If anyone ever needed to be part of something, it was him.

Once Chase buckled up, Dad drove and spoke.

"I have a lot to tell and teach you all in just a couple of hours. Tomorrow morning, I'm leaving on an early flight to Africa."

"Tomorrow?" Abby yelled. "Great. You're going to miss Christmas Again!"

"I'm sorry, Abby, but I don't have a choice. Now that I remember who I really am and what my mission is, I have to get back to work. And you three have to help me. Of course I'd rather be here decorating a tree with you and buying presents and singing Rudolph, but I really don't have a choice. This won't be like the last times I left, I promise. We may be thousands of miles apart but we'll always be close as long as you wear your amulet. Come on, we're here."

Chapter Nineteen

They stepped out of the car, walked the stone path, and entered Dad's house. In the middle of the living room sat a giant shape covered in a sheet. "What's that, Mr. McNabb?"

"A surprise, Chase. A surprise. First, come sit down, all of you."

The three children sat on the couch in front of the shape. There used to be a coffee table there, Abby recalled. She leaned over to peek under the cover but Dad stopped her. "You have to wait."

He sat on the chair next to them. "By now, you all know that pieces of Gibeon act like doorways to our world, our plane. Small pieces like the one in Abby's necklace allow communication. Large pieces like the one under the Sacrificial Table let us walk right through. Once we're on this side, we have to stay near a stone or we lose our anchor and quickly forget our Gibeon selves."

The kids nodded.

"From back on Gibeon, we plan what needs to be done to help your world. Most of the Gibeons are planners and thinkers, communicators. They coordinate messages and identify the key people who can change your world, usually a writer or politician. And some of us, the jumpers, make contact with those people. The right humans don't normally stumble across a gateway though so we jump out at places like Mystery Hill and then into any human who is close by. We tell that person to pick up a certain rock. When he does we tell him to put it in his pocket and insist that he gets it to the person we need to reach. He'll become obsessed with delivering the stone."

"Like Mimi and the governor?" Abby asked.

"Yes...exactly. I was jumping into her to tell her to get the stone to the governor. If it had worked out, when the small stone reached him, I would have tried to convince him to end the war. I'd have given him messages of peace over and over until he had to listen."

"Dad, how many gateways are in our country?"

"A lot. You'd be surprised how many gateways to Gibeon are in Massachusetts and New Hampshire alone. There's one in a local castle, another one was dropped accidentally in a restaurant. We placed them all over the place thousands of years ago so we'd never get trapped anywhere."

"But you got trapped anyway," Claudia said. "Do they all get stuck in humans that run away too quick?"

"No. Some jumpers do get stuck accidentally when they're spreading peace messages. But many, too many, go into people just for fun, with no message to deliver. It's against our laws but they don't care. Sometimes it's for minutes, sometimes hours or days, but they always forget who they are eventually. And once they forget, they take over the human completely and we have to track them down and bring them back."

"If it's against the law, why do they do it in the first place?" Chase asked.

"They hear about it from other Gibeons who have been brought back. It's like a drug. Dangerous and illegal but a lot of humans take the risk and do them anyway because someone else did. It's tragic...Tragic and stupid. Don't you kids ever do it." He got angry suddenly.

"We can't, Mr. McNabb. We're already human. We can't jump anywhere."

'Yes, that's right. Well, don't do drugs then."

"We won't," Chase said.

"Yeah, that would be really stupid," Abby said.

"Now, where was I? I was going to make some kind of point. What was it?" He tapped his fingers on his legs. "Hmm...Tap tap tap. Oh I know...The laws...Jumping. When we find the Earth Gibeons and let them remember who they are, most of them will agree to come right back. They don't mean to spend a lifetime away from Gibeon, just a little while. They just forget."

"But some of them choose to stay here, don't they?" She raised her eyebrow at Dad.

"Some of them yes, they fight it. But it's the law that they go back."

"So you'd have to force some of them wouldn't you?" Abby felt just like an attorney from TV just then. She wanted to say, "Just answer the question," but didn't.

Dad fidgeted. "Right, not all of them will want to come back. Some of them jump into people with the intention of staying in forever and they'll do whatever they can to avoid being caught. When I do find them though, I'll order them back. They know the order comes from Raphael and they won't fight it. There won't be any physical forcing. They'll come." Dad looked about as sure as Abby felt.

Abby rolled her eyes up. "If you say so..."

"I do say so." He waited but Abby didn't say anything else. He looked relieved.

"So, I will track down all the Earth Gibeons and bring them back. Raphael gave me the gift of memory so I can be human *and* remember the Gibeon plane. I'll be able to recognize an Earth Gibeon if I'm close. Maybe I always could. Remember I said before that I feel a funny flutter in my chest when an alien is close by?" The kids nodded. "Well, maybe those were Gibeons the whole time."

"All space aliens are Gibeons?" Chase asked.

"No, of course not; not by a long shot. But maybe the ones that made my heart flutter were. Since the other Gibeons don't remember who they are and won't suspect anything, I can sneak up on them. Once I'm close and they remember, it's just a matter of sending them home."

"What happens to the person underneath?" Chase asked.

"The human underneath won't realize that anything has changed. Gibeons bring confidence to humans and help them to be stronger and happier. When they leave the humans might feel a little weaker or a little lonely, but it doesn't last. Hopefully all the behaviors the Gibeon taught them over the years will stick."

"But you're not going anywhere right?" Claudia asked.

"Right...My human soul left so there's nobody to come out. It's just me."

"Will the families of the humans notice?" Chase asked.

"Probably not, it's like I said, there are a few days of adjustment but the human and the family will just think he or she is having a tired or gloomy time. It passes quickly. No harm done." Dad smiled.

"Doesn't the Gibeon get sad though? What would happen if Raphael made *you* go back? Wouldn't you miss us?" Abby knew the answer. They all did.

"But I can't go back. The human body would die."

"I said 'if!'" Yup, really felt like a lawyer.

"Yes, the Gibeon will be a little sad but once they get back to our plane, they'll be very happy. Sadness is a human emotion. On Gibeon, everyone is happy all the time." He made a big smile but Abby saw through it.

"Then why do they leave and come here in the first place?" Abby asked.

He threw his arms up in the air. "Abby, we've talked about this. They leave because it's a temptation. Being human is something different for them. Yes, they get attached to families and we feel bad taking them away from them, but there are humans underneath. That's who we need to think about. The humans underneath deserve to have their lives back."

There were tears in his eyes and Abby felt badly for giving him such a hard time. Clearly, he wouldn't enjoy ripping the Gibeons from their homes and sending them back. Why make it even harder for him?

"Sorry. You're right. We need to send them back." Abby didn't feel convinced of it in her heart, but she knew it was the right thing. Who was she to question a society that had been around since the beginning of time? She was only nine years old.

"Thank you, Abby." He patted her head and smiled at her. "But first we need to find them and make them all remember one by one."

"Mr. McNabb, can't the Gibeons just look down and see where they all are and bring them all up at once?" Chase asked.

"That would make it easier, but no. It's a complicated process getting them to return. Raphael can see them all from there but I will only be given one at a time to investigate. Because I've been human so long, I can relate to them on their level. I know what they'll go through and can do a better job convincing them to return to Gibeon."

"Andy," Claudia asked. "Are you the only dead Gibeon?"

"Dead?" he asked. "What do you mean?"

Abby saw that he was distracted by that question so tried again to peek under the sheet in front of her.

Dad pulled her hand away.

"You know, the only Gibeon without a human soul?" Claudia explained.

"No, actually I'm not. There was one other jumper who got stuck once. I don't know who the human is. Raphael says I don't need to know. But there is one other."

"How did he get a dead person? Does he know who he is too? Did Raphael let him remember?" Abby became suddenly more interested in that than in the shape on the floor.

"First of all, it's a she. And all I know is that our jumper dove into a teenage girl whose father was a novelist. It was supposed to be a quick jump to get her to pick up a stone to give the girl's father. She was near a gateway somewhere in the world, here or Scotland. India, maybe. Raphael didn't say. Wherever she was she had a fight with her boyfriend and ran off the site. She jumped in her car and sped off before our jumper could get out. She was upset and not paying attention and, well, she hit a tree and died within a few minutes."

The kids stared at dad. "So why didn't the girl, the jumper, go back to Gibeon then?"

"Well, if someone dies suddenly the Gibeon doesn't go right back to Gibeon; they get sent to a holding place. The human soul leaves right away though. Like with me, the human soul left but then the body came back. The human wasn't dead all the way. And our jumper wasn't in the holding place yet. It all happened too fast. No time to do anything."

"So what happened?"

"Well, no one knew what happened until years later. The teenager grew up, and of course forgot all about her Gibeon self. She happened to go to a gateway once with a friend and Raphael sensed her. He got her alone and talked to her, gave her the memory back and asked her why she didn't return."

"What did she say?" Chase asked impatiently.

The suspense was killing Abby too. Why couldn't he just hurry and tell what happened?

"When our jumper woke up in the hospital after her car accident she watched as the girl's parents clung onto each other, tears streaming down their faces. The girl's sister fainted in the chair from grief. Our Gibeon could have jumped out then and let the body die. She could have gone to the holding place and then to Gibeon, but she couldn't bear to see the family suffer. She said she could feel the love coming from them stronger than anything on the Gibeon plane. She said she was needed more there in that room, in that human, than anywhere Raphael could ever send her."

"Wow," Abby said.

"Yes, wow. When Raphael found her that day at the Gateway she was an adult. She said she had a new baby and a husband. She apologized to him but said she could never leave, could never go back to Gibeon because then her child would be motherless, her husband would be a widow and she would feel so much anguish when she left them, she would be no good as a Gibeon. She begged to stay, even though she was told she would forget everything."

"Did he let her stay?" Claudia asked.

"He did. He had to. To make her return to Gibeon would mean killing a human."

"Not just that, Dad, think of the family. They'd be really sad."

"They would. So she stayed and just went on with her life like that day never happened."

"Why didn't he let her remember and be human, like he's letting you?" Claudia asked.

Dad shook his head. "She didn't want to remember. It would ruin everything, she said."

"Well," Chase reasoned. "When this human body dies for good though, she'll go back to Gibeon right? After the holding time is over?"

"Yes, probably. We're not sure. It's never happened before. She and I are the only ones with no human souls. I guess when we die someday, we'll see what happens."

Tears sprung to Abby's eyes. "So you won't

be in Heaven with me when you die? I mean when I die?"

"Abby, we don't know. We'll have to wait and see. It won't be for a very, very long time. Raphael knows those things. I've been in this human body so long, I may have become human."

"So Raphael knows when you'll die but doesn't know where your soul will go?"

"Apparently not." Dad was losing his patience. Abby knew she needed to change the subject, and quick. He was right; no need to worry about anything right now. He was her dad and not dying anytime soon.

Plus that covered sheet called to her.

She grabbed the end of it and looked to Dad. "Can I?"

He nodded. "But let the others help. All of you grab an end. One- two- three!"

They whisked off the sheet.

Abby's jaw dropped when she saw the giant Gibeon monolith. It was taller than Dad and just as wide. It looked just like the stone on her amulet. Silvery-gray with lines and triangles in it. Warm tingles spread through her when she touched it.

Dad ran his hand over it too. "It's my own personal gateway to Gibeon. While I'm away finding the Gibeons all over the world, you'll have a job to do here. I'll send the Gibeons back here to go home. You'll help them with the journey."

"All by ourselves?" Claudia asked.

"Always the three of you. Always at the same time. You are never ever to try it alone. It must be all three of you, do you understand?"

The children nodded.

"But how?" Chase asked.

Dad looked at his watch. "In a few minutes we're sending someone back."

"What? Already?" Abby asked.

"Yes, already. I'm leaving tomorrow and I need to know you can do this. First, all of you hold hands and stand around the monolith." They did. "Now, close your eyes and think *open the gateway*."

Abby thought the words and could hear the others' too. The room filled with blue light and suddenly all three children floated, suspended in midair in a world of pulsating changing rainbow colors. Everything smelled like flowers and mint and chocolate and everything else wonderful they could think of. They heard thousands of voices talking and laughing.

Holding hands with Chase and Claudia steadied her or else she would have fallen on the ground. With her eyes closed, she could see Gibeon as she had seen it at Mystery Hill and in her dreams. Breathtaking. More colors than she could see with human eyes. She smiled and her heart raced. Pure happiness, that's what the feeling was...Pure happiness and peace. This was Gibeon. A tunnel of colors spun just ahead.

Dad's voice spoke in the background. He yelled over the sounds of Gibeon. "Let go. Let go of their hands." She couldn't focus but then felt her hand move. Suddenly she was back in the room.

"Wow," Chase said. "That was awesome. Better than any Six Flags or Disney ride ever."

"Better than Universal Studios too," Claudia added.

Abby couldn't say anything. Too incredible for words.

"Now that you've all had a glimpse of Gibeon, you understand. When the three of you are together, standing around the monolith and holding hands, this is what it will be like. I'll send Earth Gibeons to you and they'll hold your hands. You will all think *open the gateway* and then the Gibeon will go down the tunnel. As soon as he or she is gone, it will close and you'll be back. Do you understand?"

Abby didn't answer. Instead she asked a question. "What was all the noise? Who were all those people? I could hear Chase and Claudia but who were the others?" Abby asked.

"Every Earth Gibeon. Every conversation and thought of every Gibeon who needs to go back."

"That's an awful lot, Mr. McNabb. You're going to be wicked busy."

"Yeah, Andy. It will take forever to catch all them." Claudia said.

"I hope not. Anyway, I can't think like that. I'll get overwhelmed. That's why Raphael is giving me one assignment at a time. Do you think you know what to do?"

The kids nodded.

"Okay, one more thing." He went into his closet and retrieved three small boxes. He handed one each to Chase and Claudia. "Here you go...Your own amulets."

"Cool," Chase said.

"Thanks, Andy. Abby, help me put this on." Claudia lifted her hair while Abby fastened the clasp.

"Dad, I thought you could only get these from Gibeon?"

"Well, yours was delivered straight from Raphael, but the others are handmade by a man named Mr. Poof. He lives on the other side of Massachusetts."

"Is he an Earth Gibeon?" Claudia asked.

"No," Dad said smiling. "He's just a human artist. The amulets you're wearing were very expensive and have a lot of Gibeon in them. Please don't lose them."

"We'll be careful, Mr. McNabb."

"Plus you won't be able to do your job without them."

"Dad, we said we'll be careful."

He nodded. "When the three of you are here, around the monolith, you can access the gateway. But if you are somewhere else and need to reach us, put your stones together. When all three stones are together it will create a mini gateway."

"How small? Can we walk through it?" Abby asked.

"No, but you'll be able to see and hear Gibeon like you just did. Whenever you want to feel the peace and happiness you just felt, the three of you just have to put your stones together and you'll be there."

The three of them stood, beaming with their Gibeon meteorite amulets.

"This is important. Promise me you'll never take these off. Promise?"

"We promise."

"What's in the other box? Is that another amulet? Who's it for?" Abby asked.

There was a knock at the door.

Dad looked up. "I'll explain in a minute but first I have to answer the door. This isn't going to be easy kids, so be ready. I didn't think he'd come so early but he's here now and we have to send him back. Please trust me that this is what has to be done okay?"

"Sure Dad, we trust you." Abby said.

Abby was scared as heck but today was the most amazing day she had ever had in her life. Even when her dad left to go to Africa and all around the world to find Earth Gibeons, Chase, Claudia and she could go to their own private special place, their little slice of paradise. Yes, she was scared, but she wouldn't give up this experience for anything.

"Okay kids. I'm going to open the door and I need you to stay focused. We'll only get one chance at this... Just one. You have to be strong."

"We will," they vowed.

Abby, Chase and Claudia crowded around Dad. Abby couldn't' believe they were sending someone back so soon. She didn't feel ready but trusted that Dad would guide them in what to do.

Dad finally opened the door and Abby gasped when she saw the Earth Gibeon. Claudia's eyes bugged out, and her jaw nearly dropped to the ground.

Chapter Twenty

Johnny Macaroon stood in Dad's living room. It took every bit of human courage he had not to start crying in front of everyone, especially when he saw Claudia's face. She was crying. He wasn't sure if it was because she'd be sorry to see him go or because she was mad he'd lied to her.

Johnny wiped his eyes. So much for human courage...

"Hi kids."

None of them said a word. Abby got a little teary eyed which surprised him. She'd been looking at him funny for weeks and he thought she knew. "Sorry I lied about who I was."

"You didn't know," Chase said as tears flowed down his face.

Time to fess up. "Yes, I did. I've known the whole time."

"But I thought Gibeons forgot," Claudia said.

Dad spoke. "Johnny's special. He knew."

Johnny nodded. "The human Macaroon is a good guy too. A great guy, I bet. I'm sure he'll love you kids as much as I do." He tried to wipe his eyes and whacked his glasses.

Abby looked at him. "Johnny Macaroon," she said. "I should have known. Wow. All along and you were right here... Right under our noses."

She was smart kid. She probably would have figured it out eventually even without Raphael's help.

He nodded. "I'm sorry I couldn't tell anyone. I tried to keep this from happening, Abby. I tried to keep Andy from ever remembering. I've followed him around for years, keeping him distracted from looking into Mystery Hill. I knew what would happen when he found out. I knew I'd have to go back. I thought he'd go back too. I didn't know he was in an empty body. I'm glad I got to know you though."

"Why?"

He smiled at her. "You're my niece, silly."

"Niece?"

"Your dad is my brother."

"You're Mr. McNabb's brother?" Chase asked.

"Not Mr. McNabb's...no, I'm the Gibeon Andy's brother. His big brother." He smiled with tears in his eyes. "It's been great getting to know all of you, but I've got to do the right thing and go back now. You do what your dad tells you, Abby. It's okay that I'm going back. Gibeon is a great place. You kids help him okay?"

Abby's heart felt like it was being ripped out. She had always had a funny feeling about Johnny. He was an odd duck and she never particularly trusted him. But a Gibeon? She knew she had to send him back but, well, it would be like losing two dads. He'd been around so much and she'd gotten used to his quirky ways. Her real

Dad would be traveling all over the world and Johnny? He'd be out of this world. The human Johnny Macaroon wouldn't be the same.

And how did Dad feel? Imagine having to send your own brother back. She'd been giving Dad such a hard time and had no idea what he must have been going through. She didn't like this job one bit. Didn't like what it did to the Gibeons, or what it did to their human families. A terrible, terrible thing.

Johnny looked at her and smiled. Her uncle. Her uncle since the beginning of time. "It's okay that I'm going back," he said. Did he mean it? She looked deep into his eyes.

Underneath lived a man who had his life stolen from him. The human Johnny Macaroon hid underneath, trapped, probably dying to get out. Johnny was right. They had to send him back.

"I'm glad I got to know you too," Abby said. She wiped her eyes. "We'll miss you."

He smiled and reached way down to kiss her cheek. "You take care of your dad too. I won't be here to watch him anymore."

"Mr. Macaroon, will you talk to me sometimes?" Chase asked. Looked like Abby wasn't the only one who was losing a father figure. She didn't even know Chase liked Johnny much less would miss him.

Johnny hugged Chase then looked him in the eye. "Don't you worry about that. I'll stay in touch."

Dad opened the third box and took out a shiny amulet. It was round like theirs but had swirls of gold and chips of diamond on it. It swung on a shiny chain. He handed it to Johnny to put on.

"How come he gets one?" Claudia asked through tears.

"So I can keep an eye on you," Johnny said, tapping her wet nose. "Andy and Raphael thought it would be a good idea if all the Earth Gibeons put one of these amulets on before they went back. Then we can watch our old human families and make sure everything's okay and talk to them sometimes. It'll make the transition easier."

"It's pretty," Claudia said.

Johnny smiled. "Sure is. Andy found a great website that sells some beautiful things, amulets and rings... lots of nice stuff. All the Earth Gibeons will get one so we won't feel so sad about leaving. We'll always be close to our friends, the people we love."

Claudia held up her amulet. "If you ever want to talk, I'll be here."

"Me too," Abby said. He smiled and took her hand. "Come on, let's do this."

Claudia took his other hand and they joined Chase around the monolith. Dad stood in the background, guiding them.

They all closed their eyes and thought, *open the gateway*.

And then the Gibeon Johnny Macaroon was gone.

Chapter Twenty-One

May—Six Months Later

It was hot for May. Darn hot. Abby dripped sweat. Claudia and Chase leaned against a tree in the shade. Mom yelled, "Okay, it's ready!" She pushed a button and the sprinklers went on. Chase ran through first, then the girls followed suit. The cool water soothed her.

It also felt good to have life back to normal again. Well, it would never be the way it was, but Abby finally adjusted. Winter had been tough. No doubt about it. This had been the hardest but best year of Abby's life. The human Macaroon was nice and was still a toy inventor. He was confused for a few days, didn't come around much but then was fine. Of course he didn't do weird things like stalk Dad's house anymore and he had lost a lot of weight. The chocolate and sugar obsession was purely Gibeon.

He didn't ever talk about the other Johnny, didn't seem to know he had been taken over by someone else for a long time. He had a girlfriend now and the Candles and McNabbs didn't see him as much as they used to. But that was best for him, Abby figured. Little by little he was drifting out of their lives.

Dad was gone for the most part, chasing Gibeons around the planet and sending them to

Bradfield for the kids to send home. The first few times were scary but they got used to it. With the exception of Johnny Macaroon, there had been no emotional journeys. All the others who had passed through the gateway at Acorn Hill were strangers to them who loved to opportunity to go back, once they remembered.

Dad and Abby spoke every night through her amulet. Though he traveled far away, they had never been closer. Finally, she understood him. Finally, he said, she believed him and he couldn't be happier. Gradually Dad began telling her about his life before Andy McNabb, about other places he had lived. Tales of stars and planets and planes without names or times, filled their nights. His stories fascinated her and Abby had what she had always wanted: To be truly proud of her father.

Claudia had grown up a lot since the fall. Johnny's going back hit her pretty hard, rattled her down to the core. She hadn't been nearly as close to him as Abby had but she just couldn't get over the look on his face before he passed through the gate. And because Claudia was clearly the most sensitive one in the group, it became her job to ease the Gibeons into the house and through the gateway. She calmed them all down and made them excited about their return. Claudia handed them all amulets before their journeys were complete, let them know they could watch over their families and lend a hand if needed. Once the Gibeon passed through, she told the confused humans that the amulet was a good luck charm they needed to wear. Claudia explained simply that it was a love stone and if they wore it, they'd always feel love. And wouldn't you know it, all the humans left there smiling, utterly charmed by the little blonde girl.

She communicated with them for as long as she needed to until their emotional transitions were complete. She threw herself into the job and it fit her. Claudia had found her niche: helping people. Or aliens as the case may be. Abby had to admit that she was amazing when it came to nurturing. She was a natural. That winter, Claudia had found her purpose. She said someday she was going to be a psychologist.

Chase had changed too. His parents had always pretty much ignored him because they were so caught up in their work. He had spent his childhood dealing with it the best he could. Once Johnny passed over though, he suddenly saw how much Chase was hurting. Since Gibeons existed to comfort and help, Johnny became Chase's surrogate dad. He talked to him every night through the amulet. Chase told Johnny his dreams, his hopes. He had someone to talk to about school and life. Finally, Chase told Abby, someone really cared about him.

Johnny promised Chase he'd come back some day. Become a physical being again and be by his side. It didn't surprise Abby that Johnny planned to jump back to Earth as soon as he was able. It did surprise her that she didn't divulge that to her

Dad.

Some Gibeons were meant to live here. And not all rules made sense.

Abby doubted Johnny would be able to get back again, but just hoping he could gave Chase hope. He was different a kid now. Outgoing, happy. Proud.

Chase turned into a junior executive. He ran the business end and was in charge of making sure all the Earth Gibeons got their amulets. He had an open account with an online jewelry store who supplied him with all that he needed. Now and then Dad would request a paperweight to be anonymously delivered to a politician. Ordering and delivering those larger chunks of Gibeon was Chase's job too.

Mostly, he was the one who formally took care of "Mr. McNabb's fish." Chase had keys to Dad's place and justification to go there every day. There were no fish of course, but it gave them all a reason to go to Dad's. Lily, George and Saffron never suspected a thing when the children went there.

The kids checked Dad's writing website daily just incase anyone needed any other kind of paranormal help. Dad said he couldn't give up that part of his life just to be a soul collector. He couldn't abandon his fans or the people who needed him. Writing new books would be tough but he said as he traveled to collect souls he gathered up more paranormal facts than he could write in a lifetime. He promised to get the kids increasingly involved as they got older.

Abby ran through the sprinkler again...So refreshing. Things were good. She peered over into the woods. Even they weren't scary anymore. The scarecrow tree grew more leaves and now looked a lot friendlier. Before Dad left for Africa he collected all the twig houses and spider web sculptures and tossed them in the garbage. "Don't need these anymore," he said.

Chase ran by Abby, water dripping off her face. "Abby, guess what?" He had his hand on his amulet.

"What," Abby laughed, thrilled to be cool.

"Johnny came back. He's back!"

"Chase, he can't come back." Abby frowned.

Just then, a deep woof-woof came from the woods. A hugely fat bulldog huffed and puffed from behind a tree. Abby laughed. He looked just like Johnny but short and without glasses. He sat at Abby's feet and seemed to smile with a big wrinkled, drooly mouth.

Abby was about to tell Chase again that it couldn't be Johnny but there was something there, in his eyes. She remembered what they used to promise Dad. "We believe everything." She reached down to pet the dog and noticed Johnny's Gibeon medallion around his collar. Maybe...

"Hey, isn't that the new dog Johnny Macaroon just got from the shelter?" Claudia asked.

Chase laughed. "Yeah, and apparently Johnny

doesn't want him anymore. Strange huh?"

The kids looked at each other and laughed.

"Yeah, strange that he gave his amulet to his dog too," Abby said, grinning.

"Come on, Orson," Chase said, guiding the dog through the sprinkler. "Looks like I got myself a dog."

Orson looked back and winked at Abby.

"No Gibeon laws about animals," Chase explained.

Claudia ran to the water and hugged the pooch. "Welcome home Johnny. I mean, Orson."

He looked at Abby and wagged his tail. She laughed. It was Johnny all right.

Abby giggled and ran through the water again then hugged Claudia. Chase caught up with them, smiling.

The three humans held hands and ran through the sprinkler with their amulets glistening in the sun, reminding them that magic was all around them. All they had to do was believe.

The End

The Truth

Though much of the material contained in this book is fiction, much of the data in this book is true. *Too much to ignore.*

The Facts

America's Stonehenge, also known as Mystery Hill, exists in Salem, New Hampshire only miles from the Northern border of Massachusetts. Despite decades of research by many archeologists, there is no solid answer as to who built the site or why. Many opinions state that it is truly 4,000 years old.

When the site was built, Arcturus and Izar (part of the Boötes Constellation) were distinctly bright Zenith stars. According to Professor Louis Winkler, the broken monolith where our Andy McNabb sat marked Izar's grazing circumpolar star.

Four billion years ago a star with no name exploded. A Supernova sent bits of this star hurtling through the universe for billions of years. Though *opinions* vary on times, most *facts* state that about forty million years ago it crash-landed into Namibia, Africa in an area called Gibeon. Much later, man was created and for thousands of years, they used pieces of this dead star to build weapons.

In 1838, James Alexander first collected pieces of the Gibeon meteorite and sent them to a chemist in London for identification.

Could the Gibeon meteorite be present at America's Stonehenge? Could its high metal content be the source of metal that supports the Tectonic Strain Theory? Probably not as that's a long way for pieces of it to travel, but what if?

There is no evidence of a star called Gibeon in any books of astronomy, but could it have been part of the Boötes constellation? Could pieces of it still float in the Bootids Meteor shower? If so, are there still Gibeons living there, waiting to someday fall to a planet where they can help to create joy? It's certainly fun to dream about.

The biggest fact, one that cannot be denied, is that there are many people who believe in aliens and in other dimensions. Many people who feel out of touch with this world and who seek answers to life's mysteries and those of the Earth. There are many people who wonder endlessly about places like America's Stonehenge, the Bridgewater Triangle, the Desert of Maine, haunted restaurants and houses, and eerie wooded areas where innocent sculptures made of random sticks are anything but innocent and random...

Many people will read this book and wonder if the connections I've made could be plausible. Look at the facts and decide for yourself.

I'd like to thank www.furthers.com for their sale to me of my Gibeonite rings (which inspired this book) and the amulets I purchased for my real-life Abby. Chris Ploof is a talented artist.

I'd also like to thank the owners of America's Stonehenge for providing a beautiful setting for a book and an intriguing mystery to be solved.

There are many books and websites dedicated to the research of the Gibeon Meteorite and America's Stonehenge a/k/a Mystery Hill. Many opinions, many theories, many facts. Read, explore, discover... And most of all don't be afraid to believe.

Below are some sites I found helpful in my research:

The Gibeon Meteorite:
http://www.alaska.net/%7Emeteor/GNinfo.htm

The June Bootids- Meteor shower:
http://spaceweather.com/meteors/junebootids.html

Site about Boötes Constellation:
http://starryskies.com/The_sky/constellations/bootes.html

Official website for America's Stonehenge/Mystery Hill:
http://www.stonehengeusa.com/indexold

Other helpful Mystery Hill website:
http://www.unmuseum.org/mysthill.htm

Interesting books:

America's Stonehenge: The Mystery Hill Story **by David Goudsward, Robert E. Stone and Malcolm Pearson**
http://www.amazon.com/Americas-Stonehenge-Mystery-Hill-Story/dp/0828320748/ref=sr_1_2?ie=UTF8&s=books&qid=1213634236&sr=8-2

Ancient Stone Sites of New England and the Debate Over Early European Exploration **by David Goudward and Niven Sinclair**
http://www.amazon.com/Ancient-England-Debate-European-Exploration/dp/0786424621/ref=sr_1_3?ie=UTF8&s=books&qid=1213634377&sr=1-3

Tracy L. Carbone lives in Massachusetts with her daughter and a house full of pets. She writes in her spare time, mostly late at night or on the train as she commutes to her day job. **Man of Mystery Hill: An Abby McNabb Mystery** is Tracy's first published children's novel but she has sold several short stories in the US and Canada. Tracy enjoys spending time with her daughter Abigail, light of her life, on whom the character Abby McNabb is based. Besides writing, Tracy loves to cook, make homemade jams, and any kind of crafts. Her favorite activity of all though is cuddling on the couch in front of the fireplace, typing stories into her MAC, with her little dog Anna by her site. She is a member of NEHW, HWA and Sisters in Crime.

Please visit her website for more details about her writing, or to contact the author at

www.tracylcarbone.com
or
www.abbymcnabb.com

Made in the USA
Charleston, SC
14 September 2010